Enid Blyton's
STORYBOOK

Published by World International Publishing Ltd.
under the Young Wordsworth imprint.
All rights reserved.
Copyright © 1992 World International Publishing Ltd.,
an Egmont Company, Egmont House, PO Box 111,
Great Ducie Street, Manchester M60 3BL.
Printed in Czechoslovakia.
ISBN 0 7498 0691 5

CONTENTS

Swing High!

Swing high –
Up and down!
Point your shoes,
Strong and brown.
Touch the leaves,
Touch the grass.
Catch the pigeons
As they pass!

In the park
High on the hills,
Bright with flowering
Daffodils;
Over the church, with a
Clock of gold . . .
Swing, until
You're very old.

When your beard
Is long and grey:
Eighty Springs have
Swung away!

AMELIA JANE AND THE SAILOR DOLL

Once a new sailor doll came to the playroom where Amelia Jane and the rest of the toys lived. He was such a chatter-box.

"You know, sailors have adventures, plenty of them," he said. "And you should just hear mine . . ."

"We don't want to," said Amelia Jane. "You've told us about twenty times already."

"You're the rudest doll I've ever met," said the sailor doll huffily. "Well, as I was saying, one day when I was out at sea in my ship—I was the captain, of course—an enormous storm blew up, and the ship rocked to and fro, to and fro, just like a . . ."

"Rocking-horse," said Amelia with a giggle.

"Please be quiet," said the sailor. "Well, I somehow steered the ship to land and everyone was saved. Another time I went out in a lifeboat to rescue two people who couldn't swim. I got a medal for that. Look."

"It's not a medal," said Amelia Jane. "It's a button you picked up at the back of the toy cupboard. It's been there for ages."

"I don't believe you've ever *been*

day came when the children took the toys out into the garden for a picnic. They took little chairs and tables, too, for the toys to sit on, and gave them tiny cups of lemonade and plates full of biscuit crumbs. The toys really enjoyed themselves.

After the picnic, the children went indoors and left the toys by themselves. They were beside the little round pond where water-lilies floated on the water. Amelia Jane wanted to take off her shoes and paddle in the water. She called to the sailor doll.

"Come on, Sailor! You love the water, don't you? Let's paddle up to our knees, and you could take off your suit and have a swim, if you wanted to."

"I don't want to," said Sailor.

"You could sit on a water-lily leaf and have a very nice time," said Teddy.

"Don't be silly," said Sailor.

"Well, just come and wet your toes," said the golliwog. "Come on, you're always talking about what a wonderful life it is on the water. Here's plenty for you!"

in a ship or a boat," said the clockwork mouse. "You just talk and talk."

Well, the sailor doll wasn't going to stand any rudeness from the mouse, and he chased him all round the room and smacked him hard. Then he made a face at Amelia Jane and turned his back on her. He began talking all over again.

"*How* can we stop Sailor from going on and on about adventures I'm sure he never had?" said the teddy-bear. "He's like a gramophone that won't stop."

Well, Sailor went on like that till a

"I'm sleepy," said the sailor doll. "Leave me alone. I wish there was somewhere soft and cosy to curl up on—I'd have a nap in the sun."

Amelia Jane stared at him and a wicked look came into her eyes. "I know what you can do!" she said. "Look!"

She took hold of a toy table and turned it upside-down. She took some small cushions off the toy chairs and tucked them into the upside-down table. It looked a bit queer with its four legs sticking up into the air.

"A nice cosy bed for you!" said Amelia to Sailor. "Get in and have a nap. You *do* look tired."

Sailor was surprised to have so much kindness from Amelia Jane. He got into the table-bed and lay down. He yawned loudly. "Nobody is to disturb me," he said.

"No your majesty," said the clock-work mouse with a giggle.

Sailor frowned and closed his eyes.

"Don't disturb him," whispered Amelia Jane to the others. "Let him go fast asleep."

They were all puzzled. Why was Amelia being so nice to the sailor doll? Nobody liked him much. "I'll tell you in a minute," she whispered.

Soon the sailor doll began to snore. He often snored, and usually Amelia Jane stuffed a cushion over his face to stop him. But she didn't this time. She tiptoed to the table-bed and smiled all over her face. She beckoned to Teddy, Golly, and the clockwork mouse.

"We'll carry the upside-down table to the pond," she whispered. "And we'll set it floating on the water like a little boat. Whatever will he say when he wakes up?"

The clockwork mouse giggled so loudly that the bear gave him a sharp push. "Be quiet! You'll wake Sailor!"

Very gently the four toys each took one leg of the table and carried it to the pond. They set it down on the water, and Amelia gave it a push. It floated off beautifully to the middle of the pond, bumping into a yellow water-lily as it went. The goldfish were very surprised. They popped their red noses out of the water and had a good look.

"There he goes," said Amelia Jane with a chuckle. "He's got a boat at last! Hello, Captain! Hey, Captain, wake up, you're on a voyage to far away lands!"

The sailor doll woke up with a jump. He frowned. Hadn't he told the toys he wasn't to be disturbed? He turned over crossly on his cushions, and put one hand out over the edge of the floating table.

He got a sudden shock. Goodness! He had put his hand into something cold and wet! He sat up in a hurry.

He gazed round in fright. He was bobbing on the pond! Goodness gracious, what had happened! Why, the land seemed a long, long way away! He saw the toys standing on the edge of the pond, laughing.

"How did I get here?" he shouted. "Save me, quick!"

"You're the captain of your boat!" shouted Amelia. "You're sailing far away. You're having an adventure! Ooooh—mind a storm doesn't blow up!"

"I don't like it!" wailed Sailor, clinging to one of the table-legs.

"I feel sick."

"He's sea-sick," said the clockwork mouse.

"No, pond-sick," said Teddy with a grin. "Our brave and wonderful Sailor, who has been through so many marvellous adventures, feels sea-sick on the pond. Hello—here

comes the rain!"

Plop, plop, plop! Great rain-drops fell on Sailor. The wind blew a little and ripples came on the pond. The table-boat bobbed up and down, and sailed all by itself into the very middle of the water-lilies.

"Help! Help!" yelled Sailor. "I shall drown! I shall fall in and drown!"

"Swim then!" shouted Golly, enjoying himself. "Swim like you say you do when you go and rescue people."

"I can't swim!" wailed Sailor. "I can't, I can't! Save me!"

"The table's bobbing about on those little waves—I think it will turn over," said the clockwork mouse. "Why, Sailor! Your boat may sink! Get out and sit on one of those water-lily leaves—they are so nice and flat!"

Sailor really was afraid that his table-boat would sink. He jumped on to a big, flat water-lily leaf. He sat down on it—and immediately it sank

beneath him, and there he was, sitting in the water, yelling at the top of his voice.

"Goodness! He'll drown! He really and truly *can't* swim, for all the tales he's told us!" said the bear suddenly. "Look, he's slipping off that leaf— he's right in the water! I must save him!"

And, will you believe it, the fat old teddy-bear suddenly plunged into the pond and began to swim as fast as he could towards poor old Sailor! Wasn't it brave of him?

Sailor clutched hold of him and Teddy swam back, puffing and panting. All the toys crowded round. They patted Teddy on his dripping wet back, and told him he was very, very brave.

"*I've* had an adventure now!" said Teddy, trying to squeeze water out of his furry little ears. "I swam out and saved somebody."

"Yes. But *your* adventure is a true one and Sailor's never are," said Amelia Jane. "Are they, Sailor?"

Sailor was standing all alone, his clothes making a puddle of wetness round his feet. He looked very much ashamed of himself. "Thank you, Teddy," he said in a small voice. "You were very brave—braver than I've ever been."

"That's the way to talk!" said the golliwog, pleased. "Come on—the sun's out again, so you and Teddy can sit in this sunny corner and get dry. Whatever will the children say if they find you dripping wet?"

Well, both Teddy and Sailor were dry when the children came back— but the little table still floated upside down on the pond! How surprised they were to see it there.

"Cushions in it, too!" they said. "What *have* the toys been up to?"

The toys didn't say a word, of course, but Amelia Jane looked even naughtier than usual.

And now, when Sailor forgets himself and begins one of his tales, Teddy interrupts at once, in a very loud voice, and begins his own tale.

"Once I swam out to rescue a silly sailor doll who couldn't even *swim*. It was a wonderful adventure for me. I'll tell you all about it."

And then, of course, Sailor stops boasting at once and creeps away. A sailor doll who couldn't swim! He will never, never be allowed to forget that.

What naughty things you do, Amelia Jane! However do you think of them?

FLOWER LANGUAGE

Everyone loves flowers, whether they are growing in a garden, park, or in the woods and fields; but how many people know that flowers have a language of their own? Each flower carries its own meaning, so that when you give a posy of flowers to someone, you are also giving them a message.

Here are some clues to this very special language.

Cherry

Cherry blossom is a symbol of intelligence, so the person you give these delicate blooms to should be very flattered.

Pansy

Pansies are a sign of thoughtfulness, and you would give these to show that you are thinking of someone.

Snowdrop

The snowdrop appears to show us that Spring will soon be here, and the message of this little flower is one of hope.

Tulip

The bold, brightly-coloured tulip is a symbol of fame, and the flowers themselves are certainly famous all over the world.

Violet

The shy violet is the opposite of the tulip, and its name means modesty.

Rose

This popular flower carries a popular message too. The rose is a symbol of love, and it is enjoyed by all as one of the most beautiful of all flowers.

Some very special beaks

Like its wings and tail, a bird's beak is specially designed for its way of life, and as different birds live different lives, then their beaks must be different too.

Take the little sparrow, for instance. He likes to eat seeds and grain, so his beak is short and thick to help him to crush them up.

The swift spends so much time in the air that he even eats up there, and as he flies along he opens his beak to catch any insects, moths or beetles in his path.

The woodpecker lives up to his name – he pecks wood – so his beak is strong and pointed. Once he has chiselled a hole in the bark of a tree, he pushes his long tongue into it to catch the hidden insects.

The shoveller lives up to his name too. He is a duck and his food is found under the water, so his beak is big and heavy so that he can push it along, collecting tiny plants and animals and sieving out water.

Another bird who feeds in the water is the heron. The heron's beak is long and pointed, like a dagger, and he uses it to spear fish. He wades through the water on his long legs, and then suddenly strikes.

The crossbill feeds mainly on the seeds of pine cones, and his beak is adapted so that he can remove the seeds as he moves along the branches. The crossbill is so named because the tips of his beak cross over.

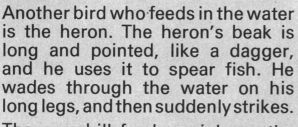

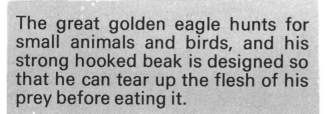

The great golden eagle hunts for small animals and birds, and his strong hooked beak is designed so that he can tear up the flesh of his prey before eating it.

Finally we have the oystercatcher, who lives on shellfish like oysters, mussels and cockles. His beak is long and pointed, and he uses it to prise open the shells before eating this tasty food.

17

Growing plants from pips and leaves

Plants can be grown from the seeds of grapefruit, lemons, oranges, pomegranates, dates and peaches. Always select pips and stones from fruit that is fully ripe as these will be most likely to shoot. Soak pips or stones in water for three days before planting.

Place an orange, lemon or grapefruit pip one cm deep in a small flower pot containing garden soil. Keep it in a warm dark place until the first shoot appears. Now put it on a sunny windowsill and keep it watered. When it has grown two pairs of leaves, transplant it into a larger pot.

Your miniature tree will never bear fruit, but the foliage is attractive in the house. If growing several plants, label each pot with the name of the seed and the date so that you will know how long they take to germinate.

Plant a date stone three cm deep and water regularly. This leafy palm resembles an aspidistra.

If you plant peanuts in their shells crack the peanut case gently to help the nuts to shoot easily. Place two in each pot, just covering with soil. The shoots appear within three weeks and tiny clover-type leaves develop.

You can grow pips more quickly

months. Keep the soil moist, but do not over-water.

Balance an acorn in the neck of a small jar filled with water, and when root develops transfer it to a pot containing soil or peat. A miniature oak tree is most decorative.

Bury a 'conker' five cm deep in a large pot buried in soil in the garden. The pot prevents it growing into a giant tree.

Grow a peach tree outside near a sunny wall. It will soon become a healthy plant and need training up the wall.

If you fancy a sycamore tree, detach one wing from a seed and bury it in soil with the seed-vessel downwards.

Another way you can grow plants is from leaf-cuttings. Many indoor and outdoor plants, including the African violet and gloxinia, can be propagated in this manner. Plant cuttings during March-April or August-September.

You require a small brown pill bottle so that little light penetrates inside. Choose a healthy leaf from an African violet plant with about an inch of stem and a tiny "knuckle".

Fill the bottle with water and cover with foil by tucking this over the bottle edge. Pierce a hole and push the "knuckle" into the water, which must be kept topped-up.

After several weeks roots will appear. When one cm long, plant in a pot and keep indoors. Water the soil each week as leaves appear but never wet them or they will rot and fall off. If lucky, the plant will grow large dark-green leaves and violet, pink, blue or white flowers, according to the species.

Experiment with other leaves to find which will grow in this way.

by placing them in soil in a polythene bag. Seal this by tying at the top and put in a warm place or a sunny window. Keep in the bag until the third leaf appears, then plant in pots and keep in a warm room.

Raspberries, strawberries, blackcurrants and other fruits can be grown. Wash the flesh from the pips in a cup of water, then dry on blotting-paper. Place the pips just below the surface of moist potting compost or sandy soil.

Apple, pear, cherry, avocado pear and even unroasted coffee beans will sprout if well-soaked in water before planting. Some stones germinate quickly but others take a few

THE TALE OF TWISTY AND HO HO

"The cows shall drink out of this stream," he said. "They will be thirsty, walking all the way home this hot day."

Now, as Ho-Ho stood watching the sparkling water, he heard the sound of someone whistling, and he turned round to see who was coming. He saw Twisty the gnome coming along swinging a big stick as he went.

"Good morning, Twisty!" called Ho-Ho. "Where are you going?"

"I am going to the market to buy my master some sheep," said Twisty, "and this is the stick I have cut to drive them home!"

Once upon a time Ho-Ho the Goblin went along by the fields to catch the bus that went to the market. He walked by the stream, and sang as he walked, for it was a very pleasant day.

Ho-Ho was going to buy some cows for his master. He was to bring them home that evening. He had cut himself a big stick from the hedge, and with this he meant to drive the cows home. Ah, Ho-Ho felt very important to-day! He stood still for a moment and looked at the bubbling stream.

"Now that is a funny thing," cried Ho-Ho. "I am going to the market to buy my master some good cows that will be sold there to-day. And I have cut this stick to drive them home! We will catch the bus together, buy our animals together, and come home together!"

"Yes," said Twisty. "And my master said to me, 'Twisty,' he said, 'see that you give the sheep a drink on the way home, for they will be very thirsty walking so far on the dusty roads.' And when I saw this stream I thought to myself that this would be where they drank."

"No," said Ho-Ho at once. "They cannot drink here, Twisty."

"And why not?" asked Twisty.

"Because my cows will drink here to-night," said Ho-Ho. "And they will be very thirsty indeed, and will drink so much that there will be none left for your sheep."

"Then you must take your cows somewhere else to drink," said Twisty. "For certainly my sheep will drink here! I will not have your cows drinking from this stream, for, if they do, there will not be enough water for my sheep!"

"I tell you your sheep shall *not* drink here!" shouted Ho-Ho.

"And I tell you that your cows shall not drink here!" Twisty shouted back.

Ho-Ho banged his stick on the ground, and the dust flew up. "If you bring your sheep to this field, and let them drink from this stream, I shall drive them away," he said.

Twisty hammered his stick on the ground, and the dust flew up in such a cloud that Ho-Ho began to choke. "I tell you, Ho-Ho, if you bring your cows here to-night I shall push them all into the water!" shouted Twisty.

"Indeed you will not!" yelled Ho-Ho. "If you do, I shall hit you with my stick—like that!"

With that he struck Twisty with his stick, and the gnome howled with pain. He lifted his own stick and hit out at Ho-Ho. He knocked his hat off, and it fell into the water.

"There goes my best hat!" groaned Ho-Ho, and he stamped on the ground in rage. He poked Twisty hard with his stick, and the gnome over-balanced and fell splash into the stream!

He sat up in the water and shook his fist at Ho-Ho, who was standing on the bank laughing loudly. Out of the water jumped Twisty, shook him-self like a dog, and jumped at Ho-Ho. Over and over on the grass they rolled, and at last down the bank of the stream they went together, *splish-splash* into the water. How they choked and spluttered as they lay in the water trying to get out!

"I've swallowed a fish!" said Twisty.

"I've swallowed two!" said Ho-Ho. "And see how wet I am!"

"So am I," said Twisty. "Let us get out and dry our clothes before we go to market. It will never do to go to market dripping wet."

So they climbed out of the stream and sat on the grass in the sun. They took off their coats and hung them on a tree nearby to dry.

And, as they sat there, drying, they heard on the road not far off the *rumble-rumble-rumble* of the bus. It was on its way to market, the only bus of the morning!

"The bus! The bus!" shouted Twisty, and he jumped to his feet. "Come, quickly, Ho-Ho, or we shall lose it."

They tore off over the field and

came to the gate as the bus passed. It stopped when the driver saw them, and the two ran to it; but even as they took hold of the rail to pull themselves into the bus they remembered something.

Their coats! They had left them drying on the tree—and in the pockets of their coats was the money their masters had given them to buy the cows and the sheep! They could not go to market to buy without money.

"Wait a moment for us," begged Twisty. "We have left our coats in the field."

The gnome and the goblin raced over the field and took down their wet coats.

They turned to go back to the waiting bus, and Twisty said: "Well now, just you remember, Ho-Ho, on no account are you to bring your cows here to-night to drink from my sheep's stream!"

"What do you mean!" shouted Ho-Ho. "I told you I had chosen it for my cows, and that you were not to bring your sheep!"

Just as they stood glaring at one another they heard a *rumble-rumble-rumble*—and the bus had gone on down the lane! It would not wait any longer, for it was already late. It had gone, and the two quarrellers were left behind.

They stared at the disappearing bus in dismay. It climbed the hill and went over the top. They could not get to market that morning.

"I shall have no cows to bring to the stream to drink," said Ho-Ho, in a small voice, "and my master will be very angry with me."

"And I shall have no sheep to bring to the stream to drink," said Twisty, "and my master will be so angry with me that I shall have no dinner and no supper."

"Why did we quarrel?" said Ho-Ho. "The stream is big enough to give water to all the sheep and cows in the market!"

"We were selfish!" cried Twisty. "We each wanted the whole stream for our animals, and now we have no animals to bring to the stream. It serves us right. Good-bye, Ho-Ho. I am going to tell my master that I have missed the bus."

"Good-bye," said Ho-Ho. "I must go back to the farm, too. Next time we meet, Twisty, we will be more sensible."

But somehow I don't think they will—do you?

A day
by the
SEA

In the wild, blustery wind
My kite goes flying . . .

In the heaving, falling tide
My ship goes sailing . . .

In peanut-salty pools
Tiny shrimps go swimming . . .

Along the sandy shore
I go running . . . *running!*

The WILD FLOWER Fairies

When you go for a walk through the woods and fields, I am sure that you see many wild flowers, but I wonder if you know that some of these flowers are the homes of little fairies, each one with a special task to perform.

The Red Poppy Fairy

If you look carefully at the inside of the red poppies which grow in the cornfields during the summer months, you will see that inside the flower there are lots of little black stamens.

You might think that these are part of the flower, but in fact the Red Poppy Fairy has been helping the Fairy Chimney Sweep to empty his sack into the middle of each flower, and then she turned the soot into part of the poppy by weaving a magic spell.

The Pansy Fairy

It is the job of the little Pansy Fairy to take her palette of white, yellow, mauve and purple paints, and paint 'faces' on her own special flowers. The wild pansy is also known as the 'heartsease' and whenever country children are naughty, they usually go and pick a bunch of wild pansies as a peace offering for their mummies!

The Scarlet Pimpernel Fairy

Another of the wild flower fairies has a very important job. She is Fairy Scarlet, who looks after the scarlet pimpernel flower which grows from May to November in gardens and fields. You see, whenever the rain fairies tell Fairy Scarlet that it is going to rain, the little flower fairy has to fly around quickly and pass on the news to all the scarlet pimpernel flowers, because these flowers are called 'The Poor Man's weatherglass' and they always close their petals tightly at the first sign of rain. And because of this, country people have come to rely on the flowers to tell them the state of the weather. So Fairy Scarlet must never forget to tell even one pimpernel . . . or else the weather forecast would be wrong, and that would never do, would it?

The Ragged Robin Fairy

It is the task of some fairies to clear up the litter from the countryside, but the Ragged Robin Fairy collects the moulting feathers of the robin redbreast. She turns them into the flower which bears her name by dipping them in the magic stream. But the water makes the feathers damp and this gives the flower a rather ragged appearance . . . hence its rather unusual name!

The Dock Fairy

Have you ever wondered why you can usually find the dock plant growing near a patch of stinging nettles? It is because of kind Fairy Dock who knows how horrid it feels to be stung by a nettle, and so she plants lots of docks nearby which have the magic power to take the nasty sting away quickly.

So if you are ever stung by a nettle, look for a magic dock leaf to rub on the wound to take the sting away. Fairy Dock will most certainly have planted one for you somewhere nearby.

ALL THE YEAR ROUND

JANUARY is the very first month of the year. It is the middle of winter, the nights are long, and the weather is very cold. When it snows, you can put on lots of warm clothes and go sledging, or make a snowman, but don't forget that the birds can't find food in the snow, and will need the food that you put out for them.

FEBRUARY is another cold winter's month, but the first flower of the year braves the weather and shows her face. The little snowdrop, or "Fair Maid of February" as she is called, brings the first sign that the winter is almost over. There are pancakes to look forward to on Shrove Tuesday, and February 14th is St Valentine's Day.

MARCH brings the end of winter, and the evenings start to get lighter. Daffodils and crocuses bloom, buds appear on the trees, lambs are born, and although the March winds blow, you know that it won't be long before the spring is here.

APRIL is the month of showers, and you will need to wear your wellingtons and raincoat when you go out. However, the rain and the mild weather bring more spring flowers, and up in the trees you will hear the song of the cuckoo. Birds are building their nests, and you can pick bluebells and primroses in the woods to make a spring posy.

MAY brings warmer weather, and the swallows fly back to spend the summer here. The hawthorn blossoms in the hedgerows, earning its name of the Mayflower, and in the fields you will find the first daisies. Soon the baby birds will be born, and their parents will have to work very hard to feed them.

JUNE is a true summer month, with hot sunny days, warm light evenings, and the scent of roses everywhere. Midsummer's Day, the longest day of the year, is on June 21st, and rumour has it that all through that night the fairies are dancing and feasting. Bees and butterflies hover over the flowers, and the air is full of the songs of birds.

JULY is the time for outdoor games, especially as the school holidays have begun. You can go for picnics in the woods and fields, fish in the stream, or play games in the park and your faces will soon be brown with all that sunshine. There are summer flowers everywhere, but there are also nettles, so be careful.

AUGUST is another holiday month, and many people go to the seaside. You can go swimming, build sand-castles, or go exploring, while overhead the sea gulls float on the sea breezes. This is also the harvest month, and all over the country the farmers are gathering their crops with the help of their big machines.

SEPTEMBER heralds the end of the summer, and sadly you go back to school. Now the fruit is ripening on the trees, the swallows prepare to fly to warmer lands for the winter, and the nights are getting longer. Soon the leaves will turn from green to bright orange, red and gold.

OCTOBER brings the autumn, with falling leaves and cool breezes. The apples and pears are ready to pick, and there are lots of conkers to be found under the Horse Chestnut trees. The hedgerows are full of ripe blackberries, shiny red hips and haws, and plenty of nuts for the squirrels to store away.

NOVEMBER starts on a cheerful note with Bonfire Night, and the darkness glows with the light from many bonfires and fireworks, while you enjoy the baked potatoes, treacle toffee, and parkin. Animals are frightened by the bangs, so make sure that your pets are inside. There are plenty of autumn leaves to be swept up, and soon the trees will be quite bare.

DECEMBER comes, and the winter is well and truly here. Still, there is Christmas to look forward to, with all the excitement of making and wrapping up presents, decorating the tree, collecting holly and mistletoe, singing carols, and finally the big day itself. In fact you are so busy, and are having such a good time, that you don't even think about those warm summer months.

HE BORROWED A TEAPOT

Jinky was giving a tea-party. He had asked Tiptoe, Mr. Tumpy, little Rubbalong and Silky the pixie. So it was to be a very nice party indeed.

He was busy setting out the tea-table in his little sittingroom. "Five plates, five cups and saucers, teapot, jug and sugar-basin," said Jinky.

He called his little servant, Peepo. "Peepo, have you finished cutting the sandwiches? Oh, good. Put the honey sandwiches there, and the jam ones there. And have the buns cooked yet, and that lovely chocolate sponge cake?"

"Just ready, just ready," said Peepo, hurrying here, there and everywhere.

Dear, dear, what a to-do, to be sure, when Jinky gave a party!

The buns were whisked out of the

oven, done to a turn. The sponge cake was perfect. The crackle-biscuits were so light that Peepo hoped the wind wouldn't blow them off the plate.

"Lovely, lovely!" said Jinky. "Now, here come my guests, Peepo. You can make the tea, and please remember to make it of fresh dewdrops, it tastes *so* much nicer."

Peepo picked up the pretty teapot with its pattern of pink-tipped daisies, and hurried to make the tea. Her foot caught in a rug—and down she went! The teapot flew out of her hand, crashed against the wall, and then fell to the floor.

It smashed into a hundred tiny pieces. Peepo gave a loud wail. "Oh, it's broken! Oh, Jinky, have you enough magic to mend it! Oh, dear, oh, dear, I'm so sorry."

Jinky ran into the kitchen in dismay. "Oh, my—I haven't nearly enough magic to mend all *those* pieces together!" he said. "We shall have to borrow another."

"But who from?" wailed Peepo. "You want such a big one for a party like this. Dame Tricky has one, but her lid is broken, and you can't have a broken teapot for a party."

"Well, here come my guests," said Jinky, and he turned to greet them all. He told them about the broken teapot. "I suppose none of you have one to lend me?" he said. "A nice big one!"

Nobody had. But Tiptoe had a good idea. "You know that little house not far from here?" she said. "Well, a little girl lives there, and she's sure to have a toy tea-set. Her teapot would be *just* the right size for us. Perhaps you could borrow it, Jinky. I'm sure she wouldn't mind."

"Good idea!" said Jinky, and he ran straight off to the little house.

He flew up to the window-sill and looked in at the playroom. What a bit of luck! The little toy teaset was set out on a small table near the dolls' house— four plates, four cups and saucers, the teapot, the jug and the sugar basin.

33

"Now I shan't have to look for it," said Jinky and he flew into the room and down to the floor.

He looked round for the little girl. Tiptoe had told him her name was Sarah. Sarah was nowhere to be seen —and nowhere to be heard either, which wasn't surprising because she had gone to meet Jane, her friend, and bring her back to tea.

"Well, if she's not in, she won't mind my borrowing the teapot!" thought Jinky. "She may not even know. Anyway, I would have asked her, if she had been here."

He picked up the teapot, which was exactly the right size for him, and flew off with it. He soon arrived at his little home with it, and handed it over to Peepo.

"And don't you dare to drop *this* one!" he said to Peepo.

She was very, very careful, and soon the teapot was full of lovely tea, made of fresh dewdrops. It poured very nicely indeed, and everyone said it was a great success.

"Well, now I'd better take it back again," said Jinky, after tea. "Have you washed it, Peepo? Thank you. Well, I won't be long, everyone."

Off he went, and was soon standing on the window-sill, peeping in. And, oh dear, how dreadful he felt!

There were two little girls in the room, and one was crying. That was Sarah. "I left it here, all ready for our dolls' tea-party," she said. "It was my nicest toy teapot. Now it's gone."

"But, Sarah, who can have taken

it?" said Jane, her friend. "I mean, no one would want to borrow a *toy* teapot!"

Jinky was frightened. What a dreadful thing he had done! He had spoilt Sarah's dolls' tea-party—and she thought her teapot was stolen! Would she be very cross with him if he told her who had borrowed it?

But just then he had to dart behind a spray of ivy and hide because Sarah's mother came in. "Come along downstairs and have tea," she said. "Haven't you found your little teapot yet, Sarah? Never mind—come and have tea, and perhaps you'll find it afterwards."

Mummy, Sarah and Jane went out of the room. Jinky peeped inside again, wondering what to do. *Some*how he had to put things right and make up to Sarah for upsetting her. He flew down into the room and looked at the set tea-table.

"What have they put on the plates for the dolls to eat?" he wondered. "Why—just beads! How queer! But, of course, they haven't any cakes or biscuits small enough to set out on such a tiny table."

Then Jinky had a wonderful idea. He flew straight back to his guests, carrying the teapot again, and told them everything.

"And do you know what I've thought of," he said. "Why shouldn't we make some proper dewdrop tea in this teapot, and take some of our own tiny sugar lumps for Sarah's basin, and the cakes and biscuits and sandwiches that are left over from our own tea— and put them on the plates belonging to Sarah's own teaset? Why, she's only put *beads* on each plate!"

"That's a fine idea," said Mr. Tumpy. "Where's a paper bag? I'll pack up the sandwiches for you. Silky, you pack up the cakes and biscuits.

Peepo can make the tea."

"And I'll get the sugar lumps," said Tiptoe.

"I'll help you carry everything," said little Rubbalong.

It wasn't long before Rubbalong and Jinky were upon the window-sill of Sarah's house again. Rubbalong had no wings, so he had to climb up the ivy, but he managed quite well.

There was nobody in the nursery. They were all finishing their tea downstairs. But Sarah was still sad about her teapot!

Jinky and Rubbalong were very busy upstairs in the playroom. They set the teapot full of hot dewdrop tea down on the table. They put the tiny sugar lumps in the basin. They put the cakes and sandwiches and biscuits on the plates, and put the beads back into the bead-box.

"It looks fine," said Rubbalong, at last. "It makes me feel hungry all over again! Let's get back to our own party now, Jinky. You've done all you can."

So back they went—and two minutes later Sarah and Jane came upstairs to the playroom, wondering how to give the dolls a party if they hadn't got a teapot to pour out their tea for them.

They came into the room, and Sarah suddenly caught sight of the teapot standing in the middle of the tiny table. "Oh, it's come back!" she said, in delight.

Then both girls saw the cakes and sandwiches and biscuits.

"Sarah! Did *you* put all these darling little cakes out—and these teeny-tiny sandwiches—and oh, do, do look at these biscuits!" cried Jane.

Sarah stared as if she couldn't believe her eyes. "No," she said. "No, I didn't put anything out at all, except beads for pretend-cakes. Oh, Jane, where did all these things come from?"

"And how did the teapot get back?" said Jane, lifting it up. "SARAH! It's full of tea. Look!"

She lifted up the lid and showed Sarah the tea inside. It was still steaming hot. The two little girls stared at one another in excitement.

"Do you know what *I* think?" said Sarah, at last. "I think some pixie or brownie must have come and borrowed our teapot, and when he brought it back, left these things—a payment for his borrowing."

"I think that, too," said Jane. "Oh, Sarah, what a good thing your dolls can't eat these lovely things. Can I have one of the sandwiches?"

Well, Sarah and Jane ate everything. They said the sandwiches, cakes, and biscuits tasted better than anything they had ever eaten before, and as for the dewdrop tea, well, it wasn't a bit like tea.

"More like magic lemonade," said Sarah. "I *say*, Jane,—we never saw these tiny sugar lumps. LOOK!"

They didn't ase those at teatime. They kept them as sweets, and they are taking them to school to-morrow. There is one for every child in the class. If you belong to Sarah's class, you'll have one, too. And fancy, you'll know how it got into Sarah's sugar-basin—and Sarah doesn't!

IN THE COUNTRY

THE SQUIRREL

This lively, bright-eyed creature lives in the woods and parks near our homes, so if you look very carefully when you are out walking you may just catch a glimpse of him.

Squirrels live in trees, eating acorns, beechnuts and leaf buds, and leaping from branch to branch using their bushy tails to balance them. They make stores of nuts so that they won't go hungry in the winter, but they make so many that they often forget where they all are. They eat the nuts by splitting them neatly down the centre, but young squirrels find this very hard to do at first.

THE HEDGEHOG

Although the sharp spines on his back make him look fierce, the hedgehog is a harmless creature. Like the fox he prefers to move around at night, and during the day he sleeps under bushes and in the hollows at the base of trees. His favourite diet consists of insects and worms, and he can move quite fast when he wants to. He can even climb walls and fences, in spite of his short legs.

When he is in danger he rolls himself up in a ball so that his spines stand out and all the unprotected parts of his body are safely tucked in. When the winter comes the hedgehog hibernates, which means that he goes into a deep sleep until the warm weather returns.

THE FOX

Another menace to the farmer is the cunning fox, who steals the hens and geese from the farmyard. He is also an enemy of the rabbit and the mole. With his keen sense of sight, smell and hearing he can hunt in the dark, so he usually lies low during the day.

The fox lives in a lair, with a female fox or vixen, and his cubs. The vixen is a very good mother, and will face any danger, or run any risk for the cubs. The fox will dig his own lair if he must, but he prefers to use an old burrow that has been abandoned by rabbits or badgers.

THE HARVEST MOUSE

This little fellow is very pretty, isn't he? He is only 2½'' long, and is so light that he can climb the stalks of corn without them bending over. His tail is about the same length as his body, and he wraps it round the stalk to help him keep his balance.

In the summer he builds a little nest which hangs from a stalk of corn, and he lines it with leaves and petals to keep him and his family warm. In the winter the cold winds blow through this nest, so the harvest mouse moves into a haystack where he lives very comfortably.

THE RABBIT

The rabbit is a timid creature, and he spends much of the day in his burrow, or warren, coming out from dusk to dawn to feed. The rabbit's warren is a very complicated affair, with lots of passages and chambers where he and his many brothers and sisters can be safe. There may be more than a hundred rabbits in some warrens.

He eats grass, leaves of plants, and unfortunately he is very fond of vegetables, which makes him un-popular with farmers and gardeners.

THE MOLE

You probably won't see a mole on your travels, because he lives under-ground, and only comes to the surface when water is a bit scarce. Also, the mole has very weak eyes, so that the darkness of his burrow suits him very well. He uses his nose and his strong front legs to dig with, and he makes a series of tunnels in the earth, leading to his cosy, leaf-lined chamber.

The mole eats worms and grubs, and so when these are in good supply he makes a store so that when he feels a bit hungry he hasn't far to go. When he makes a burrow near the surface he leaves little piles of earth on the ground. These are called 'molehills' and you may have seen them on your daddy's lawn.

SILLY-ONE AND ARTFUL

Once upon a time Silly-One, the pixie, went for a picnic all by himself. He had a package of meat sandwiches, some jammy buns, a bar of chocolate and a bottle of lemonade, so he was going to have a very good picnic.

He sat down in a nice place. A small pond was just by him, and a green hedge was behind him. The sun shone on the water, and many flies danced about over the pond.

Silly-One undid his sandwiches. He took them out and began to eat them. There was a bit of meat in one that he didn't like.

"You taste nasty," said Silly-One, and threw it away into the pond. It lay there on the surface, and didn't sink.

Silly-One looked for it in a moment or two and was most surprised to find dozens of tiny black tadpoles feasting on the bit of meat. They were swimming about round it, pulling at it, and having a fine time.

"Look at that now," said Silly-One. "I never knew that tadpoles liked a bit of meat before. I'd like to take some home and keep them. I could give them a bit of meat every day."

He dipped his hand in and tried to catch the tadpoles. But they swam away fast. Silly-One went on with his dinner, and threw another bit of meat into the pond. At once a swarm of little black tadpoles, wriggling their tails behind them, swam to it and feasted on it.

It was fun to watch them. Silly-One looked at them whilst he finished his sandwiches. Then he ate his jammy buns, his bar of chocolate, and drank his lemonade out of the bottle. He had forgotten to bring a cup.

"I'd like to take some of those tadpoles home, I really would," he said, and wondered how to get some. He took the empty lemonade bottle and held it in the pond. As it filled with water several tadpoles swam into it too.

Silly-One was delighted. He took the bottle out of the water and held it up.

"Aha, little taddies—I have six of you!" he said. "I'll take you home and

put you into my goldfish bowl and feed you on bits of meat each day. And you'll grow into giant tadpoles, so that I shall have to dig a pond in my garden for you to live in!"

He didn't want to go home just then. He stood the bottle in the shade and lay down. "I think I'll have a little nap," he said. "Just a little tiny one."

So he shut his eyes—but very soon he felt something crawling over his face, and he sat up in a hurry. It was a caterpillar!

"Oh you funny leggy creature!" said Silly-One. "Why do you crawl over me? Oh, my goodness, what a lot of you there are on that plant. No wonder you dropped on to my face! I laid myself down just under you!"

He liked the caterpillar. He liked the way it crawled about quickly on his hand.

"I've a good mind to take you home too," he said. "Yes, I have! I haven't any pets, and I think six tadpoles and six caterpillars would be nice pets. I could dig up the plant you were feeding on, and take that home, too. I could put it in a pot, and then six of you could feast all day long. How would you like that?"

The caterpillar didn't answer. It seemed in a great hurry.

Silly-One got busy. He dug up the whole plant. He took six caterpillars, and popped them into the cardboard box he had brought his sandwiches in. He made little holes in the lid so that the caterpillars could breathe.

Then, carrying his bottle of tadpoles in water, his plant, and his box of caterpillars he began to make his way home.

On the way he met Artful the brownie. Artful was always trying to make Silly-One come and live with him and do his work. But Silly-One didn't want to. So he wasn't very

pleased to meet Artful on his way home.

"Hello!" said Artful. "Been for a picnic?"

"Hello," said Silly-One. "Yes, I have. Goodbye."

"Don't be in such a hurry!" said Artful. "What have you got in that bottle?"

"Tadpoles," said Silly-One. "Goodbye."

"And what have you got in that box?" asked Artful.

"Caterpillars," said Silly-One. "Goodbye."

"Now look here, anyone would think you wanted to get away from me," said Artful, annoyed.

"I do," said Silly-One. "Goodbye."

Artful was angry. "I think you're a very, very silly pixie," he said. "Here

am I always offering you a good home and wages, if you'll come and do my bit of work for me, and you just won't come. You're silly. Silly by name and silly by nature."

"I may be silly, but I'm not com-

ing," said Silly-One. "And what's more, you can't make me. You don't know enough magic to make a hen lay eggs!"

"Oh, don't I?" cried Artful, in a fine rage. "Well, I'll prove to you I'm a very powerful brownie, see! I'll use strong magic. I'll frighten you so that you'll come and be my servant in case you get changed into a black beetle or something."

round your head and frighten you!"

"You're not to do anything of the sort," said Silly-One. "I don't like moths. Some people do, but I don't. They scare me. I know it's silly, but they just scare me. You leave my caterpillars alone. Anyway, you couldn't do it. You're only boasting. It would need very strong magic to change these leggy caterpillars into beautiful moths, with wings and feelers. Don't be silly!"

"I will, I tell you!" said Artful, and he took a little wand out of his pocket. He waved it over the lemonade bottle and over the box of caterpillars.

"Abra-cadabra, abra-cadabra, rimminy-romminy-ree!" he said solemnly. "There! Now they will change into frogs and moths. You'll soon see, Silly-One. Just a matter of weeks, and you'll know how strong my magic is!"

"Goodbye," said Silly-One, and fled. He didn't believe in Artful's magic at all, but it made him feel uncomfortable.

"Don't you worry," he said to his tadpoles, when he filled his old goldfish bowl with water, and popped them in. "Don't you worry! You won't be changed into frogs. Artful's magic is no good!"

He put the plant he had brought home into a pot, and then placed the six caterpillars gently on it.

"There!" he said. "Have a good feast. You are my pets now. You won't be changed into anything. You needn't believe in Artful's silly magic."

Silly-One got fond of his queer pets. He fetched water-weed from the pond for his tadpoles, and he gave them a bit of meat each day. He watered the plant his caterpillars fed on, and was pleased to see them growing bigger and bigger.

Then one day he noticed that his tadpoles had grown a little pair of back

"Pooh," said Silly-One. "Goodbye."

"Now look here," said Artful, and he caught hold of Silly-One's arm, nearly making him spill his tadpoles. "Now look here, I'll use my magic, and I'll change those nice, wriggly tadpoles of yours into frogs!"

"No, don't!" said Silly-One, in alarm. "I don't like frogs. They make me jump when they suddenly leap high in the air. Don't you dare use any magic on my tadpoles! Anyway, I don't believe you know enough! It would need very strong magic to turn taddies into frogs!"

"And what's more," said Artful, speaking right into Silly-One's ear in a most mysterious way, "and what's more, Silly-One, I'll change those caterpillars of yours into moths! See? Into yellow moths that will flutter legs each! He stared at them, and he didn't like it.

"Look here," he said to them. "You mustn't grow legs. Dear me, don't say that Artful's magic was real magic after all. Oh, don't grow legs, little tadpoles!"

But they did—and they grew front legs too! Silly-One was frightened. Frogs had four legs—and now his tadpoles had, too! It was queer, very queer.

Then something happened to his caterpillars. They didn't seem well. They wouldn't eat. They all made themselves funny little cases, and tucked themselves in and went to sleep there! They couldn't be seen. Only their sleeping-cases were left.

"Funny!" said Silly-One, quite alarmed. "I do hope they wake up soon. They'll starve if they don't crawl out and eat!"

One day the cases moved. Silly-One watched in excitement. Now his caterpillars would come out again and eat. They had had a long, long sleep!

But, oh dear, what a dreadful shock he got—for when the cases let forth what was in them—it wasn't caterpillars! It was six moths, lovely yellow moths, with long swallow-tails.

Silly-One stared and stared at them. Tears came into his eyes. "You've turned into moths, and I don't like you

any more!" he wept. "Artful's magic has changed you after all. My lovely fat caterpillars have gone."

And then he saw that his tadpoles were no longer wriggling black taddies, but tiny frogs. Yes, very very little ones, with no tail, four little legs, and a froggy mouth. They sat on the weed at the top of the goldfish bowl, and Silly-One almost expected them to croak.

There was a knock at the door, and in came Artful, smiles all over his face. He saw the moths and the tiny frogs, and smiled even more.

"Well, wasn't my magic powerful?" he said. "Didn't I turn those tadpoles into frogs, and those caterpillars into moths? Ha, I guess you feel afraid of me now, Silly-One."

"Goodbye," said Silly-One, and tried to push Artful out of the door.

But the brownie wouldn't go.

"Oh, no," he said, "Oh, no! I haven't finished my magic yet. I'm going to change *you* into something now, Silly-One! What would you like to grow into? A moth—a frog—a bee —a beetle? Just tell me, and I'll wave my wand."

"No, no!" cried poor Silly-One. "Don't wave your wand at me. You are too clever, too powerful, Artful. I will come and work for you. Anyone who can change tadpoles into frogs and caterpillars into moths is a very

great enchanter. I am afraid of you. Take me for your servant and treat me well."

"All right," said Artful, putting his wand away at once. "Come to-morrow. And mind—no nonsense, Silly-One, or you'll find yourself growing wings and feelers, and you'll be a moth flying round my lamp at night!"

Well, poor Silly-One is still Artful's servant. He didn't know that tadpoles always change into frogs, and caterpillars always change into moths or butterflies. He was such a silly one.

But you knew, didn't you? You'd have known it wasn't Artful's magic! Still, it does seem like very queer magic, doesn't it? How *do* tadpoles change into frogs, and caterpillars into moths or butterflies?

I don't know. Nobody knows. So perhaps it *is* magic!

A BIT OF LUCK FOR THE GOBLIN

There was once a goblin who thought himself very unlucky. He was always moaning and groaning about it.

"Do I ever have any luck?" he would say. "Do I ever find a spell anywhere? Do I ever have a nice bit of magic given to me? Do I ever have a wish sent me for my birthday? No, I never do!"

"Well, dear, never mind," said his wife, who got very tired of hearing the goblin grumble and grouse. "You've a nice little cottage and me for a wife, and two good suits of clothes, and ..."

"Stop!" shouted the goblin. "Do you suppose that's all I want—a tiny cottage—an ugly little wife—only two suits of clothes—and a garden that's always wanting to be dug—and ..."

"Now, what's all this?" said a booming voice and who should pass by but Mister Tricky. "Grumbling as usual about your luck, goblin? Why, if you had a bit of luck you wouldn't know what to do with it! You'd lose it with your bad temper and grumbling!"

"I would not," cried the goblin. "I'd make the most of it! You should try me and see!"

"Right!" said Mister Tricky, and he

took a belt from round his waist. "Look, here's my wishing-belt. You can have it for a while. Take it in turns to wish, you and your wife. And mind you use this bit of luck properly!"

"Well!" said the goblin, and his wife gazed in delight at the red belt. The goblin took it. "This *is* a bit of luck!" he said. "I'll use it well, Mister Tricky."

"I'll come and get it back in a little while," said Tricky, and off he went.

The saucepan that was on the stove suddenly boiled over and the goblin's fat little wife gave a squeal. "Oh! The dinner will be spoilt. Give me the belt, quick, and I'll wish it all right again!"

She snatched the belt and wished for the dinner to be all right. The saucepan stopped boiling over at once. But the goblin was very angry. He grabbed the belt back.

"Fancy wasting a wish on your silly dinner!" he cried. "How dare you! We can wish for a splendid meal, silly! We don't need to worry about your stew! I wish for a roast duck and green peas!" he yelled.

At once a large dish of roast duck and green peas appeared on the table. "You're mean," said his wife. "You know I don't like roast duck. Greedy pig! Going to eat it all yourself, I suppose."

"Be polite to me, woman!" roared the goblin. "Get me a plate and a knife and fork."

The goblin's wife snatched up the red belt. "I wish the roast duck was on your head and the peas down your neck!" she shouted, angrily.

Well, the wish came true at once, of course, which was most unfortunate.

The duck leapt off the table and

balanced itself on the goblin's head, with gravy dripping down his face. The peas emptied themselves cleverly down his neck. He gave a roar and grabbed the wishing-belt.

"You silly donkey!" he cried to his wife. "I wish you *were* a donkey! Then I could ride you to market and back and save my poor legs."

Well, his wife turned into a donkey, of course, and there she stood, pawing the floor and braying "*Hee-haw*" for all she was worth. The goblin stared in horror. He waved the belt in the air.

"I wish you weren't a donkey," he said in a trembling voice.

But nothing happened, of course, because it was his wife's turn to wish.

He put it on her back. "Wish yourself back to your own shape," he begged her.

The donkey hee-hawed her wish. But it wasn't to go back to her own shape. No—she meant to get her revenge on her unkind husband.

"I wish you were a carrot!" she brayed. "A nice juicy carrot. Then I could eat you!"

And the goblin changed into a

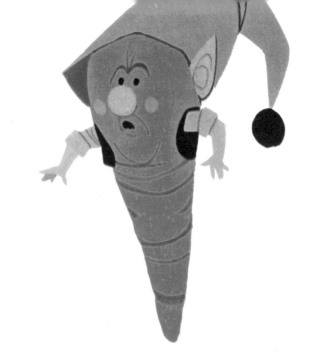

carrot, of course. It was very awkward. He lay there on the floor, and the donkey moved up to him. She bared her teeth. The carrot trembled. The donkey licked him, and then did a gentle little nibble. The carrot squealed.

The donkey kicked the carrot out of the way, not really meaning to eat him. He fell on the wishing-belt and at once he wished very hard indeed.

"I wish I was myself, I wish I was myself!" And at once he was himself again, with the roast duck on his head and peas down his neck.

He put the wishing-belt rather humbly over the donkey's back. "Please wish yourself back, wife," he said. So she did, and there she stood before him, no longer a grey donkey but his fat little goblin wife.

"We've been silly," said the goblin, and he took up the wishing-belt. "I'd better wish away the duck from my head. It seems as if it's growing there for good!"

So he did—and the duck vanished, though the peas, which he had forgotten, were still down his neck.

"What a waste of a roast duck," said his wife, who was still angry at being turned into a donkey. She took the belt, and looked at the goblin. "I wish I had two nice fat cats of my own!" she said. And at once two big black cats came and sat by the fireside.

The goblin flew into a furious temper. "Haven't I told you I hate cats? Haven't I said I'll never have them in my house? I'll wish them away again!"

"Well, if you do I'll wish them back!" said his wife. "It'll be *my* wish next."

The goblin stopped just as he was about to wish the cats away. He had a much better idea than that. He swung the belt and shouted: "I wish twenty dogs would come into the room! Then they'll chase out your cats!"

Well, no sooner had he wished than the wish came true, of course! Twenty dogs of all shapes and sizes rushed into the room. The cats at once jumped up the chimney! The dogs, sniffing the smell of the roast duck and gravy which hung about the goblin, turned to him and began to sniff at him and paw him.

The goblin's wife ran to pull them away. Then the dogs, thinking this was a fine game, began to chase the goblin and his wife round and round the kitchen. Oh, what a game they had! Over went the table and the chairs, and down went the dishes off the dresser!

"Get the wishing-belt quick, and wish!" yelled the goblin.

But one of the dogs had got it and

was rushing out of the door to play with it!

And then, in the middle of all this, in came Mister Tricky, grinning from ear to ear. How he laughed when he saw the chasing dogs and the running goblins.

"Well, well—you seem to be in a bit of a muddle," he said. "Where's my wishing-belt? Ah, I see one of the dogs has got it. Here, boy, here! That's right, put it down! Well, well, goblin, what a lot of dogs you seem to have got this morning!"

He buckled his belt round him and went to the door. "Hi, Mister Tricky!" cried the goblin, trying to push away a big dog. "Come back! Lend us your belt to wish these dogs away—and

there's a couple of cats somewhere, and I've still got peas all down my neck!"

"Keep them!" said Mister Tricky, and walked off, laughing. "I want my belt now. Ah, what did I say to you, goblin? Didn't I tell you that if you did have a bit of luck, you wouldn't know what to do with it? I was right."

Poor goblins! They still have the dogs and the two cats, because they simply can't get rid of them. But it really was their own fault, wasn't it, for wasting some really marvellous luck!

BROCK BADGER

Brock Badger is about two and a half feet long, with wiry hair which is a mixture of brown, black, grey and white; the overall effect is, however, of an animal who is black and white. He has a fine strip of white fur along his nose and a black strip crossing right over each eye and over on to his back, and he is supported by four very stumpy legs.

He doesn't seem to care *what* he eats, Brock Badger! He isn't a bit choosy. He'll enjoy anything that's around, from slugs and snails to a young bird or a honeycomb. He is a wonderful fisherman too—so you see he has no trouble surviving!

Badgers are found throughout Europe, but not too far North.

Sometimes you'll find badger houses—sets, they're called—in forests, but you are equally likely to find Brock Badger living under a flowery meadow edged with trees.

Brock's set is a marvellous bit of mining! Indeed, sometimes it has an upstairs and a downstairs, corridors, special exits for quick escapes, and lots of rooms. He keeps his set very clean—perhaps we should here include his wife—and because of this there is no unpleasant smell from it, as you might get from a fox's earth or den.

One of the most important rooms in a set is a kind of dungeon at its centre; this is a very clever bit of tunnelling and consists of blind alleys with which to trick intruders.

Badgers are courageous fighters; once upon a time countryfolk used to thrill at the cruel sport of badger-baiting.

When about to give birth, the sow retires to a special room, and the boar, the male, keeps discreetly away until it's all over. Then the sow carries her babies into the nursery — a spare room just for this purpose — and there the young ones stay until big enough to join their parents in the sitting-room! There will be between two and six babies born.

When the cubs are considered big enough to go out into the big world, they like to play *I'm the king of the castle* and *Tag*, just as children do, but whereas you might touch your friends on the shoulder, badger pups are not above giving their playmates a jolly good nip on the backside!

Remember, when next you are on a country holiday, to watch out for Brock Badger, rolling like a ship in a storm as he ventures through the forest. You may see him and his family by day, if you are lucky; but night is the more likely time. But don't forget that he has a terrific sense of smell — so keep downwind!

A Topsy-Turvy World!

*"Twinkle, twinkle, little bat,
How I wonder what you're at!
Up above the world you fly,
Like a tea-tray in the sky!"*

So said the dreamy little dormouse in the story *Alice in Wonderland*—do you remember? Being a dormouse I suppose he knew a thing or two about other sorts of mousey creatures, even ones that fly; even ones that go to sleep upside-down, like the little bat he sang so sleepily about.

Do you know anything about bats? You do—that they are very clever at avoiding bumping into things, and have webbed wings . . . and sweep through the darkness like little black elves?

There are some silly girls with long hair—and some foolish ladies too—who are afraid of bats. Afraid to go walking through the fields at twilight, through the woods after dark in case bats get tangled up in their hair. But that is nonsense. Let

me tell you why . . . and maybe one or two other interesting things about those mice of the topsy-turvy world.

When they are flying about, bats squeak. Probably about thirty high-pitched squeaks a second, except when they sense that they are nearing their prey; then the squeakings take place very rapidly indeed —about two hundred a second!

Bats have very sensitive ears. The sound they make bounces off solid objects and the interval of time between the squeak and its echo tells the bat where its dinner is!

When making these funny little sounds, a muscle in the bat's ears closes so that it can concentrate very hard on listening to the echo.

You will probably have wondered why bats hang upside down when they are asleep. Well, the answer is that they cannot *help* doing so. You see, bats' arms and legs are part of their wings so there is nothing else they *can* do but *hang upside-down* using the sharp little hooks on their toes.

Like kangaroos, bats have little pouches under their bodies and into these handy pouches they can pop their shopping—big insects that they catch on the wing, which are too big for eating all at once. But when—in June or July—the female bat has her baby, she keeps him snug and warm inside her pouch.

She needs to do this because the poor little fellow is born both blind and naked.

After a little while however, she takes him out and gives him a really good clean-up, then a fine feed at her breast, for bats are mammals, animals who must be fed on their mother's milk.

When a fortnight has passed, the little bat has a rest from clinging on to his mother's back as she flies about. Now she hangs him up by his little toes—just like a sock on the line—and there he must wait till she comes back with his dinner.

And it isn't only the Wonderland dormouse that suffers from laziness! Bats sleep three-quarters of the summer away and very nearly all of the winter, because of course they hibernate during the cold season.

Bats are big and bats are small. The great bat, the *Noctule*, is the biggest one in the British Isles and has a large wing-span. The smallest has a very nice name. It is called *Pipistrelle* and is the most common.

Never be afraid of bats! They will not hurt you, *nor* get tangled up in your hair! and like all creatures— the more you know about them, the more interesting they become.

Highdays and Holidays

Every country has special days in the year when everyone has fun to celebrate certain occasions. Here are some 'Highdays and Holidays' around the world.

The Feast of the Fish

On May 5th each year in Japan, the Land of the Rising Sun, families celebrate 'The Feast of the Fish', when from flagpoles in each garden colourful paper kite fish are flown. These kites are in very gay colours of green, red, blue and yellow, and they often glow in the dark.

The fish, which are "koi" fish as the Japanese call carp, represent strength and love, each koi representing one son of the household, and Japanese parents hope that these two qualities are shared by their sons.

The Hilarious Feast of Holi

All Indian children wait eagerly for the annual feast of Holi, for that is the day they can really have lots of fun. They wear their oldest clothes, daub their faces with red, blue and yellow paint and then they are free to wander from house to house throwing paint of every colour over everyone . . . and nobody gets scolded because it's Holi day! Actually, the paint isn't really paint at all but brightly coloured water which washes off later, but it still doesn't prevent a person getting a soaking! In order to prevent this, a few rupees are offered, which are usually accepted with glee!

The Summer Pasture Cow Parade

In the mountain regions of Switzerland children love to take part in the yearly summer drive of the cattle up to the alpine pastures. The cattle pass through all the valley villages, led by the queen cow which wears a large bell, while the herdsmen and several children follow on foot or in the carts which carry all the household utensils which will be needed by the men during their summer stay.

The Queen of Light

The 13th of December is a highday for all Swedish girls because this is the time they celebrate the festival of light on St. Lucia's Day, the day when the hours of daylight start to increase.

A "Queen of Light" is chosen who wears a crown of lighted candles upon her head and she and her chosen attendants walk around the towns and villages distributing cakes and sweets to their families, and being admired by everyone.

A Surprise for Mother and Susan

On the bookcase was a round glass bowl full of water. In it, swimming about in some strands of green water-weed, was a fine goldfish.

He belonged to Susan. She loved Goldie. She fed him, saw that he had some nice weed in his globe all the time, and once she gave him two water-snails for company. But they ate his weed so she took them out.

Goldie didn't really want company. He liked talking to the toys, when the nursery was empty. They all liked Goldie, too. He swam round and round his bowl, and sometimes he poked his nose right out of the water.

"I do wish you'd come right out and play with us!" said the sailor doll. "Why don't you?"

"Well, I have to live in water," said Goldie. "I'd like to come and play with you, really I would—but, after all, I've no legs or arms, so I wouldn't be much fun."

"You could slither along on the floor," said the sailor doll. "Do come."

But Goldie wouldn't. He didn't mind poking his nose out of the water now and again, but he didn't think he would like to get right out.

"Susan's got a toy goldfish that swims in her bath at night," the golliwog told Goldie one day. "Susan puts him in when the bath is full and takes him out again when it's empty. He lies there in the soap-rack all day and he doesn't seem to mind. If he can live out of water, why can't you?"

"I don't know. I just don't want to get out of my bowl," said Goldie, rather crossly.

"He's just silly," said the sailor doll, getting cross himself. "He won't try!"

Now when the sailor doll made up his mind that he wanted something, he went on and on until he got what he wanted! And he suddenly made up his mind that he wanted Goldie to get out of his bowl.

But how could he make him?

He thought of an idea at last. "I'll get the toys to have some sports," he thought. "Yes—running and jumping,

for prizes. I'll offer the prizes. I've got a sweet hidden at the back of the cupboard. And there's a bit of red ribbon I found in the waste-paper basket. That will do for another prize."

The toys were quite excited when they heard about the sports. The golliwog helped the sailor doll to arrange them. The toys had to run round the nursery to race one another. They had to see how high they could jump over a rope. And they had to choose partners for a three-legged race, too.

"I'll give a prize for that," said the golliwog. "I've got a brooch out of a cracker. I'll offer that as a prize for the three-legged race."

"Goldie ought to go in for the sports, too," said the sailor doll.

"Don't be silly," said the golliwog.

"He can't run. And how could he possibly go in for the three-legged race when he hasn't got even one leg?"

"But he could jump," said the sailor doll. "He could jump high out of the water. He could jump right out of his bowl! We could easily put him back. If we thought he had jumped the best, we could give him the prize. He would look nice with the red ribbon round his neck."

Goldie couldn't help feeling rather excited when he heard all this. He pressed his nose against the glass of his bowl, and tried to see all that was going on.

The sailor doll climbed up on to the bookcase. "Do you want to go in for the jumping prize?" he asked Goldie. "I bet you could win it! I once saw you jump a little way out of your water, and it was a very good jump. Don't you want a red ribbon?"

"Well, I'll go in for the jumping," said Goldie. "Yes, I will! You tell me when it's my turn."

The sports were to be held that night. The toys were excited. They started off with the running-race and the toy rabbit easily won that. He simply galloped round and came to the winning-post long before the others. He was very pleased with the sweet for a prize. It was a bit old and dirty, but he didn't mind.

"Now for the jumping," said the sailor doll. "And let me tell you, toys, that the goldfish is going in for this, too! My word, I guess he'll jump high!"

All the toys took their turn at jumping. The kangaroo out of the Noah's Ark jumped the highest of all. Goldie popped his head out of the water.

"I can jump higher than the kangaroo. I can, I can!" he called, in his bubbling voice. "Watch me!"

He jumped high out of the water—very high indeed! But alas, when he fell back, he struck the edge of the bowl, and bounced over on to the bookcase, instead of back into the water!

He slithered from the bookcase, and fell over to the edge. *Thud!* He crashed to the floor, and lay there wriggling and gasping.

"I can't breathe!" he gasped. "I

can't breathe out of water. Put me back, quickly, or I shall die.''

The toys were horrified. The golliwog rushed to him, but he couldn't get hold of Goldie, he was so slippery. And even if he could hold him, how could he possibly get him back up to the top of the bookcase?

Goldie wriggled hard on the carpet. "Water, water!" he gasped. "I'm dying! Water, get me water!"

"Sailor doll! Tell us what to do! *You* made poor Goldie jump!" cried the toys.

The sailor doll was almost crying. He had got his way. He had made Goldie jump out of his bowl. Now he wanted nothing better than to get the poor goldfish back into his water. How could he have been so stupid and unkind as to make him jump out?

"Go on, sailor doll, do something!" shouted the toys. "It's your fault, it's your fault!"

"I can't climb up to the bookcase with Goldie, I can't," sobbed the sailor doll. "He's too heavy and too slippery."

"I know what you can do! I know!" squeaked the rabbit. "Look, there is a bowl of flowers on the table. You can climb up the chair, surely, and then on to the table. Quick, pick Goldie up in your arms, and climb up. Quick, quick! He's almost dead!"

The poor goldfish was hardly wriggling at all now. He lay on the carpet, gasping, his mouth opening and shutting feebly. The toys couldn't bear to see him like that.

The sailor doll picked him up. He was wet and slippery and heavy. The sailor doll managed to climb up on to the chair seat with him, with the toys helping him. Then up on to the table he went, panting and sobbing. He ran to the flower-bowl. It was a deep green bowl and Mother had put some green

sprays in it, for there were few flowers out so early in the year.

The sailor doll flung the goldfish into the bowl of greenery. He slid down into the water. At once he felt better. He wriggled feebly at once, taking in great gulps of water, and then felt stronger.

The toys all climbed up on the table to watch. They saw Goldie flap his tail and fins rather feebly. Then they saw him wriggle himself. And then they saw him try to swim, opening and shutting his mouth as he always did.

"Goldie, dear Goldie, are you all right now?" asked the golliwog. "Do you feel better?"

"Yes. Much better," said Goldie, coming to the top of the water and poking his nose out between the stems. "But I do think it was mean of the sailor doll to make me go in for the jumping. He might have known I would fall out and crash down to the floor."

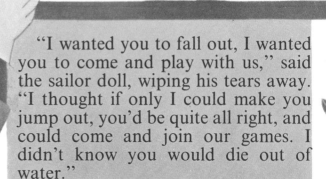

"I wanted you to fall out, I wanted you to come and play with us," said the sailor doll, wiping his tears away. "I thought if only I could make you jump out, you'd be quite all right, and could come and join our games. I didn't know you would die out of water."

"Now I'm in a pretty fix," said Goldie. "All mixed up with these stems. And the water doesn't taste very nice either. Golliwog, did I jump high? I haven't even got a prize."

"You shall have the red ribbon," said the sailor doll at once. "Come up to the top and I'll tie it round your neck. You really do deserve it, Goldie. Nobody jumped so far as you—right out of the bowl and down to the floor! Gracious, no one else would dare to jump off the bookcase."

Goldie couldn't help feeling pleased to have the prize ribbon round his neck. He felt very grand and important. He swam in and out of the stems, looking very fine.

The toys went back to the toy cupboard. The night went and the morning came. And in the morning Susan ran into the nursery. She looked at the goldfish's bowl as she always did—and stared in astonishment.

"It's empty!" she cried. "Where's Goldie? Oh, surely he hasn't jumped out and died."

But he was nowhere on the floor—nowhere to be found at all! Susan ran to tell her mother. Together they hunted about for Goldie. But they couldn't find him.

"Well, lay the breakfast, dear," said Mother at last. "Goldie's gone. Goodness knows where to!"

Susan laid the breakfast, feeling very sad. She and her mother sat down —and then her mother gave a cry of surprise.

"Susan! Look, Goldie's in the flower-bowl! How *did* he get there? Did you put him there?"

"Oh, Mummy, *no*! Of course not!" said Susan, in astonishment. "I've been very miserable about him. Mummy, he *is* in the flower-bowl—he's swimming about among the stems!"

Mother and Susan watched Goldie in amazement—and then Susan saw the ribbon round his neck. It was very limp and wet, of course, but still, it was a ribbon.

"Oh, Sue, you *must* have put the ribbon round his neck and popped him into the flower-bowl to give me a surprise!" said Mother.

And she simply wouldn't believe that Susan hadn't done it.

But Susan knew she hadn't. She looked round at her toys, and she saw that the sailor doll was wet all down the front of him. He winked at her.

"It's something to do with Sailor Doll," thought Susan. "It is, it is! But what? If only he could talk to me. Now I'll never know what happened!"

You can tell her if you ever meet her. But I'm not sure she'll believe you. Wasn't it a surprise for Susan and her mother?

The Policeman and the Angel

"Yellow is yellow,
And red is red.
But this Earth is a beautiful
Colourful ball,"
The angel said.

Orange the sun,
White the moon,
Silver the Earth
When the snow falls soon.
Blue the stars,
Red the dawn.
Yellow an Easter chick,
New-born.

"Yellow is Yellow,
Red is Red,
And Blue is Blue!"
The policeman said.

THE GOOD OLD ROCKING-HORSE

In the nursery there was a big old rocking-horse. His name was Dobbin, and he was on rockers that went to and fro, to and fro, when anyone rode on him.

He was a dear old horse, and it was very queer that the toys didn't like him! They were afraid of him—and it was all because of something that was quite an accident.

It happened like this.

One day the toy monkey fell off the shelf nearby, and went bump on to the floor. His long tail spread itself out, and a bit of it went under one of the rocking-horse's rockers.

Well, that didn't matter a bit—until John got up on to the horse and rocked to and fro. Then, of course, the rocking-horse pinched the monkey's tail hard every time he rocked over it, and the monkey sobbed and cried after John had gone to bed.

"You great, big, unkind thing!" sobbed the poor monkey, holding his tail between his paws. "You nearly squashed my tail in half. You hurt me dreadfully. I nearly squealed out loud when John was riding you. I don't like you one bit."

"Listen, monkey," said the rocking-horse in his deep, gentle voice, "I didn't mean to do that. I didn't even know that your tail was there. And in any case I couldn't help it, because John rocked me so hard. But do believe me when I say that I am very, very sorry. I wouldn't have hurt you for the world!"

"I should just think you *are* sorry!" wept the monkey. "Oh, my poor tail! Whatever shall I do with it?"

The golliwog came up with a bandage. The baby-doll came up with a bowl of water. They bathed the tail and then bound up the squashed end with the bandage. The monkey looked at his tail and felt rather grand when he saw how important it looked with a bandage round it.

It was quite better after a time—but somehow the toys really never forgave the rocking-horse, and he was very sad about it. He knew that he

couldn't have helped rocking over the monkey's tail—it was really John's fault for leaving his monkey on the floor—but the toys never seemed to understand that.

So they didn't ask Dobbin to play games with them, and they never even said "yes" when he asked them to have a ride on his back. They just shook their heads and said "no". This hurt the rocking-horse very much, because there was nothing he liked better than giving people rides.

"They think I'm unkind, though I'm not," he thought sadly. "Well, I suppose they will always think the same and I must just put up with it."

Now the toys were very friendly with a little red squirrel who lived in the pine trees at the bottom of the garden. He often used to come leaping up to the windowsill to talk to them.

Sometimes he even came right into the nursery, and he was delighted one day when they got out one of the dolls' hair-brushes and brushed his beautiful bushy tail for him.

"Oh, thank you," he said. "Thank you very much indeed. That's so kind of you. I'll bring you a present one day, Toys."

So when the autumn came he

brought them a present. It was two pawsful of nuts! He had picked them from the hazel trees for the toys.

"Here you are," he said. "Nuts for you. They are most delicious! You must crack the hard shell and inside you will find a lovely white nut. I do hope you will like them. Good-bye!"

He sprang off to find some nuts for himself. He meant to hide some in cracks and corners, so that if he awoke in the cold winter days he might find his nuts and have a meal.

The toys looked at the nuts. They were so excited and pleased because they didn't often get any presents. They longed to eat the nuts and see what they tasted like.

The golly put one into his mouth and tried to crack the shell. But he couldn't. It was much too hard. Then the brown toy dog tried to crack one. But even he couldn't! Then the toys threw the nuts hard on to the floor, but not one cracked.

"We shan't be able to eat the nuts," said the brown dog sadly. "They will be wasted!"

"Let us get the little hammer out of the toy tool-box," said the bear. "Perhaps we can break the nuts with that."

So they looked for the toy hammer and they found it. They put a nut on the floor and hit hard with the hammer. But the nut jumped away each time, unbroken. It was most tiresome.

Then the rocking-horse spoke up in his deep, gentle voice. "I can crack your nuts for you, Toys! If you will put them underneath my rockers I can rock over them and crack the shells! One of you must ride me to and fro, and then I can easily crack the nuts for you."

The toys all looked at one another. They badly wanted their nuts cracked, so they thought they would do as Dobbin said. They laid all the nuts in a row under his rockers. Then the golliwog climbed up on the horse's back and began to rock him to and fro.

Crick-crack, crick-crack went all the nuts as the shells broke. Inside were the lovely white kernels, so sweet and delicious to eat!

"Thank you, Dobbin!" said the toys. The golliwog patted him and slid down to get his nuts.

"That was a lovely ride I had!" he whispered to the other toys. "I wouldn't mind another!"

"Have as many as you like!" said Dobbin, who heard what the golly said. "Are the nuts nice?"

"Delicious! Have one?" said the bear, and he held one up for Dobbin to nibble. "It was kind of you to crack them for us—very friendly indeed."

"I'm such a friendly person," said the rocking-horse sadly, "but you won't make friends with me. I would so much like to give you all a ride."

He looked so sad that the monkey suddenly felt very sorry for him. In a trice he had leapt up on to Dobbin's back.

"Gee-up!" he cried. "I'll be friends with you! Gee-up!"

And then, one after another, all the toys had a ride, and after that they were as friendly as could be. Wasn't it a good thing Dobbin offered to crack their nuts for them?

SETTING UP AN AQUARIUM

The 'corkscrew' Vallisneria and Sagittaria are two plants very suitable for the purpose, and it is a good idea to tie a small stone to the bottom end of the plants before putting them into the tank. This makes sure that the roots will soon plant themselves firmly in the sand.

It is best to start your aquarium with the common Goldfish. These are inexpensive and require little attention, and if you study them carefully you will soon be able to try your hand at keeping the more fancy and delicate varieties, such as the Comet, Fantail, Moor, Veiltail and Lionhead.

The first thing to remember before you begin to set up an aquarium is that fish never do well unless they have plenty of room in which to swim. The ideal tank for the beginner is one about 2 feet by 1 foot by 1 foot, and it should be fitted with a hood, for some fish are good jumpers.

The floor of the tank should be covered with sand varying in depth from 1 inch in front to 1½ inches at the back. Add a few sea-shells and pieces of rock, as they help to give the fish a natural setting.

Before filling the tank with water, cut a piece of brown paper exactly the size of the tank, and lay it neatly over the sand, shells and rock. Now fill the tank with water, pouring it very slowly on to the brown paper, stopping when the water is about 2 inches from the top. Remove the brown paper very carefully without disturbing the sand, and you will find that the water will be clear and your aquarium ready for the plants.

Winter Enchantment

What can I see in winter?

HIPS AND HAWS

GREEN IVY . . .
CREEPING ON THE WALL

SNAILS ASLEEP
IN THE NICHE OF A TREE

KING STOAT, IN ERMINE,
PASSES ME . . .

AND HOLLY

CURLY KALE . . .
FOR MOLLY

MAGPIES . . .
IN THE SNOW

BUT WHERE DO THE FAIRIES
GO ?

Have fun with SEEDS

It is such fun to watch seeds growing that I am going to tell you two ways in which you can do so without planting the seeds in the ground!

For the first experiment you will need three dried peas which have been soaked in water for a day or so, three small, flat corks (or you can cut a large cork into three rounds), and a glass jam jar filled with water.

Bore a small hole in the centre of each cork, place one of the peas carefully in each centre, and put the corks on the top of the water in the jam jar. Place the jar on a windowsill. You will love to watch the three peas bobbing about on their cork boats! Each little pea will soon send out a root through the hole in the cork, and this root will drink the water and keep the pea-plant alive. After the roots have started to grow you will be surprised how quickly a little green shoot will appear!

Have you ever grown mustard and cress on a piece of damp flannel? All you will need for this is a packet of mustard and cress seeds, a piece of flannel and an odd saucer.

Soak the piece of flannel well and then squeeze the water out lightly. Put the damp flannel on the saucer and sprinkle the seeds over it. Now place the saucer on a windowsill. You will find that the damp flannel makes your little seeds grow, but some will grow more quickly than others. Soon you will see the mustard and cress begin to raise itself from the flannel because the roots will grow and lift up the seeds! When the green shoots appear, you won't be able to see the flannel at all! And how nice it will be to have your very own mustard and cress for tea!

Gypsy Caravan

It's cosy in the caravan—
The gypsy one so bright:
There's a bed for two with a quilt of blue
Of eider feathers light.

There's a cupboard filled with cups and plates;
A larder filled with stock;
A table, a kettle, two window-seats
And a wooden cuckoo-clock.

In Spring the lamps are lit at six,
In Summertime at ten.
For dinner we eat a rabbit stew;
For breakfast eggs from the hen.

The caravan is near the farm
Where our parents like to stay.
There are dens about and trees to climb
And fields where we love to play.

What tinkers lived in the caravan,
We're wondering all the while;
But the yellow wheels of our caravan—
They never turn a mile!

We're so happy in the holidays
At the caravan so bright;
With its bed for two with a quilt of blue
Of eider feathers light!

Bing Bong, the Paw-reader

Flip and Binkle had been good for a week and three days, and Binkle was beginning to find things very dull.

"Oh!" he groaned, "can't we find a more exciting job than delivering medicine for Sammy Squirrel the chemist? I hate carrying baskets of bottles every day."

Flip preferred to be good. He was afraid of Binkle's exciting ideas; they nearly always led to trouble.

"It's a *very nice* job," he said anxiously. "For goodness' sake don't give it up, Binkle."

Binkle put on his cap and opened the door of their home, Heather Cottage.

"Come on!" he said crossly. "I won't give up the job – not until we get a better one, anyway!"

The two rabbits ran across Bumble Bee Common on their way to Oak Tree Town. When they got there, Binkle saw a big notice pinned up outside Dilly Duck's at the Post Office. He crossed over to look at it. In big letters it said:

A GRAND BAZAAR
WILL BE HELD IN
OAK TREE TOWN

Binkle stroked his fine whiskers and began thinking.

"Come on," said Flip, pulling him next door into Sammy Squirrel's. "Don't dream like that, Binkle. It's time we began work."

But all that day Binkle went on thinking, and hardly said a single word to Flip. In the evening, when Sammy Squirrel paid him, Binkle gave Flip a dreadful shock.

"We shan't be here tomorrow," he said, "so I'm afraid you must get someone else to do the job."

"Oh, Binkle!" cried Flip in dismay. "Whatever do you mean?"

"Sh! I've got a lovely idea!" said Binkle, pulling Flip outside. "Come on, and I'll talk to you about it."

"I don't like your lovely ideas," wailed Flip.

"You'll love this one," said Binkle. "Listen. Did you read that notice about the bazaar outside Dilly Duck's?"

"Yes," said Flip. "What about it?"

"Well, at that bazaar there's going

74

to be Bing-Bong, who can read all your life in your paw," said Binkle excitedly. "He'll tell you what's going to happen to you in the future, too."

"Bing-Bong! I never heard of *him*," said Flip. "Anyway, what's it to do with us?"

"Oh, Flip, *can't you guess? One of us will be Bing-Bong*, and read everyone's paws!" said Binkle excitedly.

"Binkle! How can you be so silly!" gasped Flip. "You *know* we can't read paws!"

"Well, we don't need to, silly!" grinned Binkle. "We know all about everyone in Oak Tree Town, don't we? And we can easily tell them all about themselves. They won't know us, for we'll be dressed up, and they'll think we're wonderful!"

"But how can we tell them what will happen in the future?" asked Flip.

"We'll make it up!" said Binkle. "Oh, Flip, what fun it will be!"

"Will it?" said Flip doubtfully. "But look here, Binkle – you're to be Bing-Bong. I don't look a bit like a Bing-Bong person. You do; you're so

fat and big, and you've got such lovely whiskers."

Binkle twirled them proudly.

"Yes, I shall be Bing-Bong," he said, "and you can be my assistant. First I must write a note to Herbert Hedgehog, who's getting up the Bazaar."

He sat down and got pen and paper. Presently he showed a letter to Flip. This is what it said:

BING-BONG CASTLE.

Dear Sir,

"I am Bing-Bong, the reader of paws. I am passing through Oak Tree Town on the day your Bazaar is held. I will call there and read paws.

Yours faithfully,

Bing-Bong.

"There!" said Binkle proudly. "What do you think of that?"

Flip's nose went nervously up and down as he read the letter.

"I *do* hope it will be all right!" he sighed. "You do have such extra-ordinary ideas, Binkle. I don't know how you think of them."

The letter was sent, and when it reached Herbert Hedgehog he was most excited. He at once arranged to have a little room set apart in Oak Tree Town Hall for Bing-Bong to sit in and read paws.

"It *will* be grand," he said. "Lots of people will come to the Bazaar now!"

Binkle and Flip were very busy making clothes to wear. Binkle wore a purple suit with a red cloak wound tightly round him. On his head he wore a pointed hat with red stars painted all over it. He looked very grand.

Flip was dressed in baggy trousers and a little black velvet coat. He didn't like them much, for he felt he looked rather silly.

the little room at the back of the Hall. "I've put this room ready for you. We shall love to have our paws read by the wonderful Bing-Bong." And he bowed again.

Binkle looked round when Herbert had gone out.

"I'll sit in that big chair," he said. "You stand by the door, Flip. Charge a penny a time, remember."

Very soon there came a timid little knock. Flip swung the door open. Outside stood Creeper Mouse.

"Please, I've come to have my paw read," he said nervously, holding out a penny.

"Your Highness! Someone to have his paw read!" called Flip, beginning to enjoy himself.

Binkle put on some big spectacles

At last the day came, and the two rogues set out over Bumble Bee Common.

"Now remember," said Binkle, "call me Your Highness, and bow before you speak, Flip. You take the money and keep it safe. Leave the rest to me."

Flip wished he could leave *everything* to Binkle, and not go at all, but he didn't dare to say so.

"Oh my! There's Herbert Hedgehog waiting to greet us outside the Town Hall!" he whispered. "Do you think he'll see through our disguise, and know it's us?"

"Of course not!" snapped Binkle, striding forward. Herbert Hedgehog bowed very low when he saw the red-cloaked visitor.

"This is His Royal Highness Bing-Bong!" stammered Flip nervously.

Herbert stood all his prickles up very straight and made way for the two rabbits to go in.

"Very good of you to come, Your Highness," he said, and led the way to

and glared at Creeper, who stood tremblingly looking at him. He knew Creeper very well, for he was the postman of Oak Tree Town.

"Come here," commanded Binkle, "and hold out your paw."

Creeper put out his tiny little paw. Binkle stared and stared at it.

"Your paw tells me many things," he said. "It tells me that you have five brothers and sisters. You are married, and you – "

"Oh! oh! oh!" squeaked Creeper, lost in wonder. "How clever you are! It's quite true. Does my paw really tell you that?"

"Of course it does," answered Binkle. "Don't interrupt. It tells me that you walk miles and miles every day carrying a heavy bag."

"Yes, yes, I do," squeaked Creeper. "What's in the bag?"

"Your paw will tell me," said Binkle solemnly, bending closely over it. "Let me see – yes, you carry letters. You are a postman."

"Well, did you ever!" exclaimed the astonished mouse, swinging his tail about delightedly. "Oh, Bing-Bong, please tell me what will happen in my future."

Binkle looked at his paw again. "You will go a long journey, in a ship," he said gravely. "You will carry letters all your life. You will have twenty-nine children."

"No! no!" shrieked Creeper in horror, snatching his paw away. "Twenty-nine children! Why, how would I feed them all? Oh! oh! Twenty-nine children!"

And he rushed out of the room before Binkle could say another word.

Flip began giggling, but Binkle told him to be quiet.

"Ssh!" he said. "Creeper will be telling all the others at the Bazaar, and in a minute they'll all want to come and have their paws read. Hark! There's someone now, Flip."

It was Herbert Hedgehog, holding out his penny and looking rather nervous.

"Creeper Mouse says you're wonderful, Your Highness," he said to Binkle. "Could you read my paw, please?"

Binkle looked at it solemnly.

"You live in a yellow cottage," he said. "You grow very fine cabbages."

"So I do – so I do," said Herbert, in the greatest astonishment.

"You have many friends," went on Binkle, "but the two who love you best

are – "

"Who?" asked Herbert eagerly, wondering if they were Dilly Duck and Sammy Squirrel.

"They are – Flip and Binkle Bunny!" said Binkle, now thoroughly enjoying himself.

Flip's nose went up and down in delight, when he saw the astonishment on Herbert's face.

"My best friends!" echoed Herbert. "Flip and Binkle Bunny! Well, well, well! I must be nicer to them in future."

"I *should,*" said Binkle, twirling his whiskers very fast, to hide the smile on his face.

"Tell me some more," begged Herbert. "Tell me about the future."

"Er – if you dig up your biggest cabbages, you *may* find a pot of gold underneath," began Binkle.

"Fancy! Oh, my goodness! Oh, excuse me!" begged Herbert, almost stuttering with excitement. "Pray excuse me! I *do* want to go home straightaway and see if I can find that gold."

"Oh no, don't do that," shouted Binkle in alarm . . . but Herbert was gone.

"Bother!" said Binkle in dismay.

"What do you want to go and say such a silly thing for?" demanded Flip in disgust. "You *know* there's no gold under his cabbages."

"*Ssh!* There's someone else," whispered Binkle, as a knock came at the door.

It was Wily Weasel the policeman! Flip almost fell backwards in fright.

"May I have my paw read?" asked Wily politely.

"Oh – er – yes!" stammered Flip, wishing to goodness he could run away.

Wily went up to Binkle and bowed. Binkle took hold of his paw and glared at it. He didn't like Wily Weasel, for Wily had often spanked him and locked him up for being naughty.

"Your paw does not tell me nice things," he began. "It tells me that you are always hunting others and being unkind to them."

"I have to be," said Wily Weasel cheerfully. "I'm a policeman! There are lots of rogues about Oak Tree Town, and I have to punish them!"

Binkle decided to change the subject. "You are married," he said, "and you love to smoke a pipe."

"Quite right," said Wily, in a pleased voice. "Now tell me about the future. Shall I get rich?"

"Never!" said Binkle firmly. "You'll get poorer and poorer. You'll lose your job. You'll be hunted away from Oak Tree Town. You'll be put in prison. You'll –"

"Ow!" yelled Wily in terror, as he listened to all the awful things Binkle was telling. "Don't tell me any more! I don't want to hear anything else!"

He went hurriedly out of the room, groaning and sighing.

"Ooh, I *did* enjoy that," said Binkle. "That's made up for a good many spankings I've had from Wily."

Thick and fast came the knocks on the door, and Binkle was as busy as could be, telling everyone about themselves. As he knew all their pasts and made up their futures, he enjoyed himself thoroughly – till in walked someone he *didn't* know!

He was a badger. He held out his paw to Binkle and waited.

"Er – er – er –" began Binkle. "You live far away from here."

"No, I don't," said the Badger. "I live in the next town."

"That's what I meant," cried Binkle. "Er – er – you are married."

"I'm not!" said the badger indignantly. "You don't know what you're talking about! You're a fraud!"

Just at that moment there came a great hubbub outside the door and it burst open suddenly. Herbert Hedgehog came stamping in, followed by a whole crowd of others.

"I've pulled up all the lovely cabbages in my garden," he wailed, "and there's not a piece of gold anywhere! And all my beautiful cabbages are wasted! You're a fraud, Bing-Bong – that's what you are!"

"Yes, he is," cried the badger. "Why, he told me I was married, and I'm not!"

Wily Weasel strode up to Bing-Bong and glared at him.

"Are you Bing-Bong, or aren't you?" he demanded. "Were all those awful things true that you said were going to happen to me – or not?"

"Oh! oh!" wept Flip. "They weren't true, Wily; he made them up, truly he did!"

Wily turned round and looked at Flip. He grabbed off his queer-shaped hat and the green muffler that hid his chin.

"Oho!" he said, "so it's Flip Bunny, is it? And I suppose Bing-Bong is our old friend Binkle?"

Binkle decided to make the best of it.

"Yes," he said, "I'm Binkle. I only came to the Bazaar to give you a bit of fun. I'm sorry about your cabbages, Herbert. Flip, give him the pennies you've got. He can buy some more."

Everyone stared in astonishment at the red-cloaked rabbit. They could hardly believe it was Binkle who had read their paws. They had so believed in him. For a minute everyone felt angry and probably Flip and Binkle would have got a good spanking – if Creeper Mouse hadn't begun to laugh.

"He told me I'd have twenty-nine children," he squeaked. "Oh dear! Oh dear! And I believed him!"

Then everyone began laughing, and even Wily Weasel joined in.

"I'll let you off *this* time," he said to Binkle. "But next time – you just look out! Go off home, both of you. Give Herbert your pennies to buy more cabbages – and don't let me hear any more of you for a *long* time!"

Flip and Binkle scampered off to Heather Cottage as fast as they could go, very thankful to get off so easily.

And for two weeks Binkle had no more lovely ideas.

Jack and Jill went up the hill

If you were going down a hill and you saw a couple of hares, it is likely that in trying to escape they would run up towards you, then make zigzag leaps away, rather than run downhill. The reason for this is easy to find: it is because of their big back legs which are perfect for quick escape on the flat or on a rise, but much too cumbersome on a slope. So, like Jack and Jill in the nursery rhyme, you would see the hares dashing up the hill with ease, but probably Jack would break his crown and Jill come tumbling after if they both tried to escape *downwards*!

Has your mother ever said to you when you have been misbehaving —"Now get your hand out of that biscuit-tin! I've got eyes at the back of my head, you know!" She has?

Then it's quite likely that the saying came from the countryside and popped into someone's head when thinking about hares: for *their* eyes are placed very nearly at the back of their heads.

This is fine for seeing what is chasing after you or what danger is lurking behind you, but it is also a hazard, for what happens when the danger happens to be in front of you?

It is this weakness in hares that wily poachers take advantage of to gain a nice fat supper! They also know that hares are very curious creatures and that if you sit down in a field, looking as though you are much more interested in reading your newspaper than in him, a hare will, like as not, come sniffing round quite soon.

When the mating season arrives the Jack hares really *do* look mad. It's as though they do their utmost to get noticed, and the crazier they look the more likely it is that the females will sit up and show a bit of interest.

What do the Jack hares do? They run round and round the female of their choice, somersaulting now and then, coming to abrupt halts. And when they are not whizzing round the girls, they are boxing the boys— lashing out at them with their strong back legs, even leapfrogging over them! They really do intend to impress! But it is all show, for no sooner have they mated, than off they go again, crazily courting their second choice!

The females give birth to several leverets, or young hares, during the course of the year; usually two or more litters with from two to five little ones. The body temperature of leverets is unusually high, and they are born pretty advanced.

Mother Hare is a very good mother; soon she places her children in different parts of a chosen field, then gallops from one to another in order to feed them. It is never wise, perhaps she thinks to herself, to put all your little hares in one nest! And should an intruder or predator come along—*whoosh*! in a flash Mother Hare rushes up and wallops him, like a female Mohammed Ali, with her boxing gloves, those marvellous back feet of hers!

Wandering gypsies tell you hares never sleep, and that their eyes weep because of weakness. But these fine creatures aren't weak in other ways, particularly not in their means of protection, though if curiosity is said to kill the cat, it could equally kill the curious hare!

The Squeaky Doll

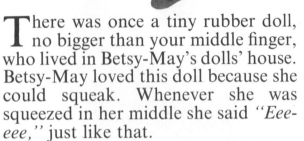

There was once a tiny rubber doll, no bigger than your middle finger, who lived in Betsy-May's dolls' house. Betsy-May loved this doll because she could squeak. Whenever she was squeezed in her middle she said *"Eee-eee,"* just like that.

But one day a dreadful thing happened to the rubber doll. Betsy-May took her out of the dolls' house to show her to Tommy, who had come to tea—and Tommy trod on her quite by accident.

And that killed the squeak in the poor little doll. She couldn't squeak any more at all. You can't think how sad she was, because, you see, it was the only voice she had.

There were three other dolls in the dolls' house, two tiny wooden ones and a little china one. They were very upset when the rubber doll lost her squeak.

"Let us put her to bed for a day," they said. "Maybe she will get her squeak back, if she rests."

So they put her to bed in one of the little beds in the dolls' bedroom, and looked after her well. But when she got up again, she still had no squeak, though all the dolls pressed her as hard as they could in the middle.

Betsy-May was just as sad as the dolls about it. She looked at the little rubber doll and squeezed her in the middle—but no squeak came.

"I don't like you so much now," said Betsy-May. "You don't seem right without a squeak."

Well, that made the rubber doll cry bitterly that night. It was dreadful not to be liked so much. After all, she couldn't help losing her squeak. The other dolls comforted her, and gave her a tiny sweet out of the toy sweet-shop.

Then they put her to bed again, and tucked her up well. They went down into the kitchen and talked about the poor rubber doll.

"It would be so lovely to hear her squeak again," said the china doll, lighting a tiny candle in a candlestick, for it was dark in the dolls' kitchen.

And just at that very moment they heard a perfectly lovely squeak. *"Eee-eee-eee!"* it went. *"Eee-eee-eee!"*

"The rubber doll has got her squeak back!" they cried, and they rushed upstairs. But no—how queer—the rubber doll was fast asleep and not squeaking at all. As the three dolls stood looking down on her, they heard the squeak again *"Eee-eee-eee!"*

And then somebody knocked quietly on the little knocker on the dolls' house front door. Down went the three dolls to see who it was.

Outside the door stood a tiny mouse. He twitched his fine whiskers and spoke humbly to the dolls.

"Oh, please, the golliwog told me you wanted a squeak, and I have a fine one. I am very, very hungry, so if you would give me something nice to eat, I will let you have my squeak."

The dolls stared in delight. "Come in," said the china doll. "I hope we *have* got something for you to eat. But I don't believe we have, you know."

The mouse went in. The dolls opened the little kitchen cupboard—but it was quite, quite empty. There was nothing to eat at all!

"Oh dear, what a pity," said the china doll. "It would have been marvellous to have got a new squeak for the rubber doll."

The baby mouse looked at the candle burning on the table. "Could I have that candle to eat?" he asked. "It is made of tallow, and I like tallow."

"Good gracious! Fancy wanting to eat a candle!" cried the dolls. They blew it out at once, took it from the tiny candlestick, and gave it to the mouse. He asked them for a glass of water. When they gave it to him he squeaked into it about twenty times. Then he put his paw over the top of the glass and gave it to the china doll.

"Let the rubber doll drink this and her squeak will come back," he said. Then off he went out of the front door with his candle. What a treat for him!

The three dolls rushed upstairs and woke the surprised rubber doll. They made her drink the glass of water. Then they pressed her hard in the middle—and she said *"EEEE-EEEE-EEEE!"* just like that. Wasn't she surprised!

"Oh, your squeak is back again!" cried the china doll. "Won't Betsy-May be pleased?"

Well, Betsy-May *was* pleased, of course—but she could never imagine where the little candle in the dolls' house had gone. *You* could tell her, couldn't you?

THE Extraordinary Chair

THERE was a dear little toy-chair in the playroom. All the toys could sit in it nicely. It was a bit tight for the fat teddy bear, and a bit big for the clockwork mouse, but most of the toy animals and all the dolls could sit down in it very comfortably.

And then Bertie, the Boy Doll, came to live in the playroom. He belonged to Pat, the little girl whose playroom it was, and when he first came, she showed him to all the toys.

"This is Bertie, my new Boy Doll," she said. "I've had him for my birthday. I want you to be nice and friendly to him please."

So, of course, all the toys *were* nice and friendly. But Bertie wasn't nice and friendly back. He took all the best things for himself!

"I want to sleep in that big cot," he said to Juliana, the curly-haired doll. "So you must make room for me too. And I want a special corner in the toy cupboard. And dear me – what a very nice chair that is – I'll have that for my own, to sit in when I am tired."

Now the little chair was a great favourite with the toys because it was most comfortable, and they all sat in it in turn. It was a wicker chair, just like the one Pat's Mummy had in her bedroom. It had no legs, but had wickerwork all round the bottom, and was nicely padded inside.

The toys were very cross with the Boy Doll. "It's most impolite of you to sit so much in our chair – you have far too long a turn in it," they said. Bertie was lazy and liked to sit down a great deal.

Well, of course, as soon as he knew it annoyed the toys to see him sitting so much in their favourite chair he sat in it all day long! Nobody could move him out because he was big and strong. What a nuisance!

And then Jummy, the little toy elephant, had a grand idea. He called the toys round him. "I say! You know that under the bottom of the wicker chair seat there is a space, don't you?" he said. "It's hidden by the wickerwork that goes round the bottom of the chair. What about me getting in that hollow space and playing tricks with the chair?"

"Oooh yes," said Juliana the doll. "Could you make it jig about and slip away from Bertie when he goes to sit in it, Jummy?"

Everyone giggled. "That would scare him," said the teddy bear.

"Let's put you under the chair now, Jummy, because Bertie has gone out for a walk with Pat. Let's see if you fit into the space beneath."

So they lifted up the wicker chair and then placed it carefully over

Jummy. It was a bit of a tight fit but quite all right!

And then the chair began to do most peculiar things! It slid along the floor by itself. It jigged up and down. It turned round and round and round! The toys laughed till they cried!

It was Jummy, the little toy elephant under the chair, who was doing it all, of course! He was walking and jigging and turning round and round under the chair, carrying it with him. But *he* couldn't be seen. It looked very queer and comical indeed.

"Sh! Here comes Bertie," said the

teddy bear, suddenly. In came Pat with Bertie. She put him down on a doll's cot and left the room. Bertie leapt off the cot and went over to the chair.

"I'm tired after my walk," he said. "I'll have a sit down."

He sat down. The toys watched. Would Bertie be too heavy for Jummy to move the chair when the doll was in it? But Jummy was very strong. After all, he was an elephant!

The chair slid along the floor a little. Bertie looked alarmed. He set his feet firmly down to stop the chair sliding about.

Jummy jigged up and down under it, and the chair hopped about a little. Bertie caught hold of the wicker arms in surprise. The clockwork mouse couldn't help letting out a little squeal of laughter.

The chair stayed still for a while and Bertie felt better. But then Jummy began to turn himself round and round and round, and the chair went too, of course – and so did Bertie! He clutched the arms in fright.

"What's happening, what's happening? The chair's gone mad! Help, help!"

"It doesn't like you," cried the teddy bear, doubling up with laughter. "Get out, Bertie, it doesn't like you!"

Bertie got out. The chair at once stood absolutely still. The toys roared with laughter at Bertie's face.

"This is silly," said Bertie. "A chair can't like or dislike anyone. The floor must be slippery or something."

"Better leave that chair alone, Bertie," said the golliwog. "It might run off with you!"

"Pooh!" said Bertie and sat down hard in it. It kept quite still. "There you are!" said Bertie. "It's quite all right now. Go away, all of you. I want a nap!"

He shut his eyes. Soon he gave a little snore. "He's asleep, Jummy," whispered Juliana. "Do something!"

Jummy did! He suddenly ran at top speed to the door, and the chair went with him, of course! Bertie woke up with a yell, clutching the arms of the chair in fright. What was happening now?

"The chair's running away with you, Bertie! It will tip you down the stairs!" shouted the toys. "Look out, look out, it's nearly there!"

But Bertie didn't get out in time, and when Jummy, still under the chair, came to the top of the stairs he stopped so suddenly that Bertie was tipped right out! He rolled bumpity-bump down the stairs from

the top to the bottom! The chair fled back to the nursery.

"Take the chair off me, quick, before he comes back!" begged Jummy the elephant. "I'm feeling dreadfully squashed. I don't somehow think Bertie will EVER sit in our chair again!"

The teddy bear lifted the wicker chair off the little elephant, laughing

NEVER going to sit in that extraordinary chair again," he said. "Never. You're right – it doesn't like me. Horrible thing! Anyone can have it now – *I* don't want it!"

And after that he never sat in the little wicker chair once. As for the chair it never behaved in such a peculiar manner again – but oh, how I *wish* I'd been there when it all happened!

till the tears ran down his cheeks. The chair stood still on the floor, and didn't move after that. Bertie came creeping back into the nursery, frightened and bruised.

"Poor Bertie!" said Juliana, with a squeal of laughter. "You look tired and frightened. Have a sit down in your chair!"

Bertie shivered. "I'm never,

THE FLYAWAY BALLOON

AUNTIE MARY gave a New Year's party to all her nieces and nephews. It was a very nice party with heaps of crackers, balloons, and things to eat.

There was one balloon that had somehow got blown up much bigger than the others. It floated with them in a great big bunch, each balloon on its own string. It was very pleased with itself.

"How big I am!" it thought. "How very, very big! Much bigger than the others. I am a Giant Balloon, and if I had a long enough string I could fly up to that big balloon in the sky – what's it called, now? Oh, yes, the Moon. I am sure I must be as big as the Moon."

It wondered which child would have it. Auntie Mary wondered, too. It was such a lovely big blue balloon, with such a nice smiley face on it that she thought it really ought to be a prize for something.

"I'll give it as a prize for musical chairs," she thought. "Whoever wins musical chairs shall have that big balloon!"

Alice won it. She was very pleased. She took the great big balloon from her aunt and held it in her arms, squashing its firm softness against her.

"It feels lovely," she said. "It's a giant balloon. It will never, never burst!"

"Burst! Whatever does she mean?" thought the big balloon. "Why should I burst? I never, never will."

And then suddenly there was a loud POP near by. Somebody else's balloon had burst. All the children jumped, and so did the balloons. What a horrid noise! and where had that balloon gone? One minute it was a lovely big yellow thing – the next it had disappeared, and all that

was to be seen was a tiny bit of dirty-looking rubber, torn and ragged, tied to the string.

The big balloon was alarmed. Was that what bursting meant? It didn't like the sound of it at all! Alice flung her big balloon into the air, holding it by its short string.

"Look – look! See how this enormous balloon flies!" she cried. "Isn't it a beauty! I'm sure it would fly like a kite if I had a long enough string and took it out in the wind."

The big balloon tried to reach the ceiling but it couldn't. The string held it back. Horrid string! The balloon wished it could get away from it.

Alice took the big balloon home. She hung it up in her bedroom at the end of the bed. The wind came in at the window and played with it, bobbing it about to and fro. It liked that.

The next day Alice took the big balloon out in the wind on its string. Aha! The wind had a wonderful game with it, and blew it quite high in the air. But the string always pulled it back.

"I might be a dog on a lead, instead of a beautiful balloon that wants to fly up to the Moon," thought the balloon, angrily. "Why doesn't Alice get me a longer string? Oh, I wish I could fly high!"

And then, next time the wind blew strongly, the balloon jerked so hard at the string that it slipped out of Alice's fingers – and the balloon at once shot high up into the air, far above the trees!

"I'm free, I'm free!" it thought, and its smiling face looked down on Alice. But the little girl was very upset. She began to cry. "You've gone! You were the biggest balloon I ever had – and now you've gone! You'll bump into something and burst. Oh, do, do be careful, balloon

– don't bump into anything sharp!"

The balloon floated higher and higher. It wanted to go to the clouds. Were they a kind of white balloon, too? And where was that Moon? That should surely be hanging in the sky like a big silver balloon. Perhaps it would come when it was dark, and then the big balloon could fly up to it, and talk to it. It was sure it would be bigger than the Moon!

The wind dropped. The balloon fell nearer to earth. Down, down,

It fell lower still. A sparrow chirruped loudly. "Balloon, be careful! That's barbed wire! It's set with sharp points. It will prick you and you'll BURST. You'll go POP and we shan't see you any more!"

The balloon just missed the barbed wire. It was so alarmed that its smiling face didn't smile any more. It began to wish it was with Alice, on a nice short, safe string!

down. It came near to a tree. Be careful, balloon – that's a holly tree. BE CAREFUL! It is set with sharp prickles! You'll burst – you'll go POP!

A robin sang out sharply: "Go away! You'll go pop-bang! Go away!"

The balloon swerved away from the holly tree. Oh dear – what a narrow escape! What dreadfully sharp prickles it had nearly floated into.

It fell to the ground and floated along, bumping up and down as it went. A rabbit saw it and ran after it, hitting it with its paw.

"Don't! You'll burst me!" cried the balloon in a squeaky rubbery, voice. The wind took it up into the air out of the rabbit's reach – but then down it fell again to the ground. This time it fell near a farm.

Two hens ran up. "What is it? Is it good to eat? Shall we peck it?"

"No, no, no! You'll burst me if you do!" cried the balloon. "Leave me alone!"

One of the hens gave the balloon a sharp peck. But it wasn't quite sharp enough and the balloon didn't burst, though it didn't like the peck at all. The other hen ran at it – but the balloon just bobbed over a fence in time. Oh dear, what a life!

It bobbed into a field where a hungry goat stood. Aha! What was this, thought the goat, and trotted up to the balloon. Something to eat? Something big and round that would make a very nice meal?

The goat put his paw on the balloon, just by the string round its neck. He bent his head down to eat it – but the wind gave a puff, and off went the balloon once more, shivering in fright. "Alice, Alice, where are you? Come and fetch me!" cried the poor balloon.

The goat hadn't burst it – but he had loosened the string at the bottom. Little by little the air began to escape out of the neck of the balloon. It grew smaller.

The wind took it along again, and, will you believe it, it blew the balloon right over the hedge into Alice's own garden! What a remarkable thing!

Alice was there and saw the balloon at once. "Oh!" she cried, running to it. "What a tiny little balloon! I never saw such a teeny-weeny one in my life! You're a baby one!"

Well! The balloon was most astonished. It didn't know it had gone small and was getting even smaller.

But it suddenly saw that Alice's hands seemed very, very big – so it knew it was now very small. It wasn't a giant any more.

Alice took it indoors and put the balloon with her brother's and sister's balloons.

How tiny it was! The others laughed at it.

"Call yourself a balloon! You're a tiddler! Wherever did you come from?"

"I was once a giant balloon," said the balloon, humbly. "I thought I would fly up to the Moon and see if I was as big as he is. But I've gone small."

"You're going smaller," said the pink balloon. "You'll soon be gone to nothing. Poor thing!"

He was right.

The balloon shrank until it was nothing but a tiny bit of blue rubber. It felt very small and humble and good-for-nothing.

"Oh! If only I were big as I was before I wouldn't boast, or grumble at my string, and want to fly to the Moon!" thought the tiny bit of rubber. "I'd be sensible. But I've lost my chance. I'm no good to anyone now."

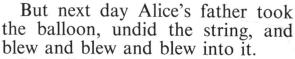

But next day Alice's father took the balloon, undid the string, and blew and blew and blew into it.

It swelled up – it got big and round and fat. It had a broad, smiling face. It was ENORMOUS!

"Why! It's the balloon I got at the party! It must be!" cried Alice. "I know its face – and it's just as big! Don't you slip your string again and fly away, balloon – you may never come back again. You may even BURST!"

"Don't worry. I'm sensible now," said the big balloon, bobbing on the string.

"I don't want to fly to the Moon. I just want to be kept on a string and be happy with what I've got."

Alice has still got it. She has blown it up five times altogether, but it's still there – and it's very, very old for a balloon, because she has had it for just over two years.

I've seen it – and I've flown it on its string.

And I do like its face. It smiles, and smiles, and smiles!

The LOST DOLL'S PRAM

"MUMMY, I do so wish Tibbles wouldn't keep jumping into my doll's pram," said Eileen. "How can I stop her?"

"Well, you could stop her by doing what *I* used to do, when you

were a baby in your pram," said Mummy. "You can put a net over the pram so that no cat can jump into it."

"Oh dear – I don't want to do that," said Eileen. "It would be an awful bother to have to do that every time I put my dolls to sleep. I shall smack Tibbles next time I find her in my doll's pram!"

Eileen found her there the very next morning, curled up under the eiderdown, fast asleep. Smack! Tibbles gave a meow of surprise, and leapt out at once. She was never smacked by Eileen and she didn't like it at all.

"You are NOT to get into the pram," said Eileen to Tibbles. "I have told you ever so often. You are a naughty little cat. Do you want to smother Rosebud or Josephine, by lying on top of them? Shoo! Go away!"

Tibbles fled away – but will you believe it, as soon as Eileen went indoors again, Tibbles jumped right into the pram once more!

She did love that pram. It was so soft inside and so cosy. She loved cuddling down, curling herself up and going to sleep in peace and quietness there.

"It just fits me nicely," she thought.

"I can share it with the dolls. They never seem to mind. They don't even kick me."

Now the next day three naughty boys came along with a naughty little girl. They saw some apples hanging on the trees in Eileen's garden, and they crept in at the gate to take some.

Eileen saw them from the window.

She rushed out into the garden. "You bad children! That's stealing! Go away and leave my Daddy's apples alone."

"Give us some!" shouted the biggest boy.

"No, certainly not. If you had come to ask my Daddy properly, he

the wall again the day after – but not to take the apples. They meant to pay Eileen out for sending them away.

"Look – there's her dolls' pram," whispered the little girl. "Let's take it away into the wood and hide it where she can't find it. That will

would have given you a basketful," cried Eileen. "But people who steal don't get any. Go away!"

"You're a horrid little girl!" shouted the boy. "We'll pay you out!"

And then Eileen's mother came out and the four naughty children ran away. They came peeping over

teach her to shout at us and send us away. Quick, Bill – there's no one about – you slip in and get it."

Bill opened the back gate, ran into the garden and took hold of the pram handles. He wheeled the little pram at top speed out of the gate. Slam – the gate shut, and the four children hurried down the lane to the wood.

"She hasn't got any dolls in the pram," said the little girl. "I'd have thrown them into the bushes if she had!"

What a very horrid little girl she was! She had dolls of her own and loved them – and yet she would have done an unkind thing to someone else's dolls! Well, well – some people are queer, aren't they?

The boys stuffed the pram into the middle of a patch of bracken and left it there. Then they went back to Eileen's garden to see what she said when she came out and found her pram missing.

She soon came out with her two dolls, meaning to take them for a walk, as she always did each morn-

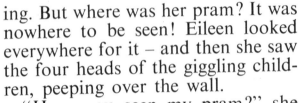

ing. But where was her pram? It was nowhere to be seen! Eileen looked everywhere for it – and then she saw the four heads of the giggling children, peeping over the wall.

"Have you seen my pram?" she called.

"Yes," they called back.

"Where is it?" shouted Eileen.

"It's hidden in the wood where you can't find it!" called the biggest boy. "Ha, ha! You'll never find it again!"

"Mummy, Mummy, come here!" called Eileen, almost in tears. But her mother had just gone out and she didn't come. So Eileen had to make up her mind herself what she was going to do.

"I must go and look in the wood," she thought. "Oh, dear – suppose it

rains? My lovely pram will be soaked. Suppose I don't find it? How am I to know where those bad children have put it?"

She put her dolls down just inside the house, ran down the garden again, into the lane and was soon in the wood. Now – where should she look?

She hunted here and she hunted there. She looked in this bush and that, but she couldn't find her pram.

"Oh, dear – there are such hundreds and hundreds of bushes!" thought poor Eileen. "I could look all day long and never find my pram. Where CAN it be?"

It was stuffed into a patch of tall bracken and blackberry bushes, and was very well hidden indeed. Someone else was well-hidden there too. And that was Tibbles!

Tibbles had been in the pram when the bad children had run off with it, curled up as usual under the eiderdown, fast asleep. When the

children had taken the pram Tibbles
had thought it was Eileen taking the
dolls for a walk. She hadn't dared
to pop her head up, in case Eileen
was cross with her and smacked her
again. So she just lay there, wondering why the pram went so fast that
morning. Then suddenly it was
pushed into the bushes, and was
still. Tibbles shut her eyes and went
to sleep again.

She woke up after a time and
stretched herself. Everything seemed
very quiet. Tibbles felt hungry and

thought she would jump out of the pram and go and find her dinner. She had forgotten that the pram had been taken for a walk – she thought she was still in her home-garden!

She poked her head out from under the covers and looked round. What was this? She was somewhere quite quite strange! This wasn't her garden. Tibbles sat right up, very frightened.

Where was she? Where was Eileen? What had happened? And dear me, was this rain beginning to fall?

It was. Big drops pattered down on Tibbles, and she crouched down. She hated the rain. She felt suddenly very lonely and frightened and she gave a loud meow.

"MEOW! MEE-OW-EE-OW-EE-OW!"

Nothing happened except that the rain pattered down more loudly. One enormous drop fell splash on to Tibbles' nose, and she meowed angrily.

The rain made a loud noise on the bracken around, and Tibbles couldn't think what it was. She didn't dare to jump out of the pram.

"MEEOW-OW-OW!" she wailed, at the top of her voice.

Eileen was not very far off, and she heard this last MEE-OW. She stopped. That sounded like a cat's voice! Was there a cat lost in the woods, caught in the rain that was now pouring down? Poor thing!

"MEEEEEEEEE-OOOOOOW!" wailed Tibbles, and Eileen hurried towards the sound. "MEEE-OW!"

"It seems to come from that patch of tall bracken over there," thought the little girl, and went to it. Another loud wail came from the spot.

"Meee-ow-ow-ow! MEE-ow-ow-OW!"

And then Eileen suddenly saw the handles of her pram sticking out of the bracken. How delighted she was! She ran to them and gave a tug – out came her dolls' pram – and there, sitting in the middle of it, scared and lonely, was Tibbles!

"Oh, *Tibbles*! It was you I heard meowing!" cried Eileen, in surprise. "You must have been asleep in the pram again when those children ran off with it. Oh, Tibbles, I *am* glad you were in it – it was your meowing that made me find it! I'll never scold you again for getting into the pram!"

She put up the hood, and drew the waterproof cover over Tibbles so that the frightened cat shouldn't get soaked. And then off she went home with her precious pram, not minding the rain in the least because she was so pleased to have found her pram again.

Tibbles couldn't imagine why Eileen made such a fuss of her, but she liked it all the same. The funny thing was that she never, never got into the dolls' pram again. She was so afraid it would run off with her into the woods and lose her!

So do you know what she does? She gets into the dolls' cot up in the playroom and goes to sleep there! I've seen her, and she really does look sweet, curled up with her tail round her nose.

THE GREEN PLUSH DUCK

THE green plush duck lived in the nursery with all the other toys. She had green plush wings, a green plush back, a red plush throat, a yellow beak and yellow legs; and a most beautiful voice that said "Quack!" very loudly when you pressed her in the middle.

Now none of the other toys had much voice. The teddy bear had only a very small growl because he had been so often pressed in the middle that his growl had nearly worn out. Emmeline, the baby doll, once had a voice that said, "Mamma!" but when Nanny trod on her by accident one day, her voice went wrong. And the golliwog never had a growl or a squeak at all, though he pretended he had.

But, of course, when the nursery was in darkness, and only the dying fire lighted up the room, all the toys had lots to say! Their squeaks, growls and "Mammas" were only for the day-time – when day was gone they used their own proper little voices, and what a chatter there was!

Now it happened one evening that the green plush duck was feeling rather grand. Paul, the little boy the toys all belonged to, had had a friend to tea, and Margaret, the little friend, liked the plush duck best of all his toys. She had let the duck sit by her at teatime, and had made her quack quite a hundred times, if not more!

So no wonder the plush duck was feeling grand. Margaret had said that her quack was just like a real duck's and that she was the nicest duck in the world. So the plush duck was quite ready to be queen of the nursery that evening!

"Did you hear what Margaret said about me?" she said to the other toys. "She said my quack was...."

"Yes, we heard it," said the teddy bear, rather crossly. "We don't want to hear it again. Forget it, plush duck."

"Forget it!" said the duck, in surprise. "Why should I forget it? I don't want to forget it, I want to remember it all my life. Why, Margaret said I was. . . ."

"Oh do stop boasting!" said the golliwog. "And don't start quacking, for goodness sake. We've had enough of that awful noise today!"

"Well, I never! Awful noise indeed!" said the plush duck angrily. "Why, let me tell you this, Margaret said that I was the nicest duck in the world!"

"Well, you're not," said Emmeline, the doll. "Margaret can't have seen many ducks, or she wouldn't have said a silly thing like that. You're not a bit like a duck, not a bit! I have seen plenty of real live ducks, and they were all white. You are a dreadful green colour, and you have a terrible quack that we're all tired of hearing, so now please be quiet."

Well, the plush duck was so angry to hear all that that she hardly knew what to say. Then she quacked very loudly indeed and said:

"So I'm not like a real duck, you say! Well, I am, so there! I can do everything a real duck can do, and I wish I *was* a real duck, so that I could live on the pond and not with nasty horrid toys like *you!*"

"Can you lay eggs?" asked the teddy bear.

"Of course not," said the plush duck.

"Well, a real duck can, so you're not like a real duck!" said the teddy.

"Can you swim?" asked the golly.

The plush duck didn't know. She had never tried.

"I expect so," she said at last. "I'm *sure* I could if I tried."

"Can you eat frogs?" asked Emmeline.

"Ooh, how horrid! I'm sure I don't want to!" said the plush duck, feeling quite ill.

"You can't lay eggs, you can't swim, you can't eat frogs, so you're not a *bit* like a real duck!" said the teddy. "Ha ha!"

"Ha ha!" said all the others.

The plush duck turned red with rage.

"I tell you I *am* like a real duck, only much nicer," she said. "I expect I *could* lay eggs and do everything else if I tried – but I've never tried."

"Well, try to lay an egg now," said Emmeline. So the plush duck solemnly sat down and tried hard to lay an egg. But it wasn't a bit of good, she couldn't. She was very disappointed.

"Well, eat a frog," said the golliwog.

"Get me one, and I will," said the plush duck. But nobody knew where to get a frog, or how to make it go to the nursery if they found one, so they told the plush duck they would take her word for that.

"Show us how you can swim," said the teddy.

"But where can I swim?" asked the duck. "There isn't a pond anywhere near, and the bathroom is too far away for us all to go there."

"You can swim in the tank belonging to the goldfish, up on that shelf there!" cried Emmeline, pointing to where the four goldfish swam slowly about in the big glass tank of water. But the plush duck didn't like the idea of that at all!

"Oh, I don't think I'll try tonight," she said. "The goldfish might not like it."

"You're afraid!" cried everyone. "You've told a story! You can't swim! You're not a *bit* like a real duck!"

This made the plush duck so angry that she at once climbed up to the shelf where the glass tank was, and popped into the water. For a moment or two she floated upright, and she was delighted.

"I *can* swim!" she called. But oh dear me, what ever was happening?

Why, the water soaked into her plush skin and got right into the sawdust she was stuffed with. And she turned over and began to sink. How frightened she was – and how frightened the toys were too!

"Help, help!" cried the poor plush duck. "I'm sinking, I'm sinking! Help!"

The goldfish nibbled at her with their red mouths. The toys watched in horror. Whatever could they do? Then who do you think came forward to help? The three little celluloid frogs that Paul floated in his bath each night! They had sat as quiet as could be all through the quarrel, because they were only small toys, and didn't like to speak. Also they had felt rather afraid in case the plush duck had offered to eat them instead of real frogs.

But they were brave, and they made up their minds to help. They jumped up to the shelf, and leapt into the tank of water. They dived underneath the poor frightened duck, and soon brought her to the surface again. The teddy and the golly pulled her out, and, dripping wet, she jumped down to the floor again.

"We're ever so sorry we teased you," said the bear, frightened. "Do forgive us."

"I'm not like a real duck," said the plush duck, sorrowfully. "I can't even swim."

"No, but you can quack," said the golly, anxious to make everything right again. "Quack, duck, and let us hear your wonderful voice."

But what a dreadful thing! The water had got into the plush duck's quack, and she couldn't say a word. Not a single quack could she quack! She *was* upset. The water was very cold and she was shivering. The toys were afraid she would catch a dreadful cold, so they took her near the fire. The teddy was very brave and poked the fire well to make it flame up.

The duck gradually got dry, but she was still sad.

"I've not even got my quack now," she said with tears in her big glass eyes. "I can't swim, I can't lay eggs, I can't eat frogs, I can't even quack. I might as well be in the dust-bin!"

"You mustn't say that!" said the toys, shocked. "Cheer up! We'll make you queen of the nursery, even if you *can't* quack!"

So they made the plush duck queen, but that didn't make her feel very happy, because she was so miserable about her lost quack.

But hip hurrah! In the morning when Paul came into the nursery to play, and pressed her in the middle, her quack had come back! "Quack!" she said, even more loudly than before! The water had dried out, and her quack was better than ever.

So now she is very happy. She is still queen of the nursery and her quack is just the same – but there's just one thing she won't do; she won't go anywhere near the tank of goldfish, and I'm not surprised, are you?

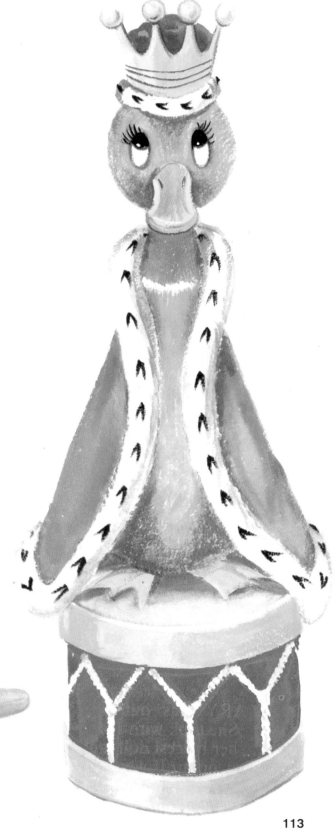

113

Mary Brown and

MARY was out for a walk. She took with her Josephine, her biggest doll, and wheeled her in her pram. It was a lovely day, and the sun shone brightly.

Mary went a long way. She walked down the little green path in Bluebell Wood to get out of the hot sun – but dear me, when she turned back, she found that she had lost her way!

Somehow or other she must have taken the wrong path – and now she

Mary Contrary

didn't know how to get back. She was most upset.

"Never mind," she said to herself. "I shall soon meet someone, and then I can ask them the way to my home."

In a few minutes she *did* meet someone. It was a little fat man in a green tunic. He was hurrying along with a white hen under his arm. Mary called to him.

"Please," she said, "I've lost my

way. Can you tell me how to get home?"

"What is your name?" asked the fat man.

"I'm Mary," said the little girl, "And this is Josephine, one of my dolls."

"How do you do, Mary, how do you do, Josephine?" said the little man, raising his pointed cap, politely.

"Yes, certainly I can show you your way home. Come with me."

Mary followed him through the wood, pushing Josephine before her in her pram. She walked down the narrow green path – and at last, to her great surprise, she came out into a little village.

What a strange village! The cottages were very tiny indeed, and at

the doors and in the gardens stood children dressed in strange suits and frocks. They looked just as if they had come out of her nursery rhyme book.

"Why, those two might be Jack and Jill!" thought Mary, looking at a boy and girl who stood holding a pail between them. "And that boy singing all by himself there is just like Tommy Tucker. Look at that tiny girl sitting on a stool too – she's just like Miss Muffet eating her curds and whey!"

"We're nearly there," said the little man.

"I don't seem to know this way home," Mary said.

"Don't you?" asked the fat man in surprise, and his hen clucked loudly

under his arm, as if she too was surprised. "Well – here you are. There's your cottage, look!"

Mary looked. They had stopped just outside a trim little cottage, whose walls were painted white. At the windows hung gay curtains, and the door was painted bright yellow. It was a dear little cottage.

"But that isn't my home!" said Mary. "You've made a mistake!"

"Well, didn't you say that you were Mary," asked the little man, in astonishment. "This is Mary's cottage. Look, there's the name on the gate."

Mary looked. Sure enough on the gate the words "MARY'S COT-TAGE" were painted.

"And look – there are your cockle shells making a nice border to your flower-beds," said the little man,

pointing. "And there are your pretty Canterbury Bells, all flowering nicely in the sunshine."

Mary stared at the cottage garden. She saw that each flower-bed was neatly edged with cockle-shells, and that wonderful Canterbury Bells flowered everywhere, their blossoms just like silver bells, instead of being blue or white.

"And there are your pretty maids all in a row!" said the little man, waving his hand to where a row of pretty dolls sat on the grass. "Look, your doll wants to join them."

To Mary's great astonishment she saw her doll Josephine getting out of the pram! Josephine walked through the garden gate and sat herself down in the row of dolls, who seemed very pleased to see her. Then the wind blew and all the Canterbury Bells

began to ring – tinkle – tinkle – tinkle!

Mary was too surprised to speak. She couldn't understand it at all – and yet she felt she had seen all this before somewhere – was it in a book?

"*Isn't* this your home?" asked the little man, looking puzzled. "Your name is Mary, Mary, Quite Contrary, isn't it?"

"No, it isn't!" cried Mary, seeing where he had made his mistake. "I'm just Mary Brown! You've thought I was some other Mary – the Mary of the nursery rhyme. *You* know, Mary, Mary, Quite Contrary. How does your garden grow, With silver bells and cockle shells, And pretty maids all in a row!"

"Well, of *course* I thought you were!" said the little man. "I'm so sorry. I've brought you ever so far out of your way."

Just then the door of the cottage opened and a little girl about Mary's age came out. She was a pretty little girl with long curly hair, and she had a big sun-bonnet on her head. Her dress reached right to her shoes and her little feet twinkled in and out as she walked.

"I say, Mary, Quite Contrary!"

called the little man. "I've made a dreadful mistake. This little girl's name is Mary, and I've brought her to your cottage thinking she lived here – and she doesn't!"

"Dear me," said Mary Contrary, in a soft little voice. "What a pity! Never mind – she had better come in and rest a little while. She shall have dinner with me, and then I'll see that she gets home all right."

Mary was delighted. She liked Mary Contrary very much indeed. It would be lovely to have dinner with her. She said good-bye to the little man who had made the mistake, and he hurried off down the street, with the hen under his arm clucking loudly.

Mary walked into the garden, and the other Mary took her into her spick-and-span cottage. It was so pretty inside – very small, like a doll's house – but quite big enough for the two children.

"It's so hot that I thought of having ice-cream pudding and ginger-beer for lunch today," said Mary Contrary, "I hope that will suit you all right, Mary."

"Oh yes!" said Mary, delighted. "I think that's the nicest dinner I ever heard of!"

Mary Contrary bustled about getting the table laid and Mary Brown helped her. Then they sat down to the largest ice-cream pudding Mary had ever seen – and do you know, they finished it between them! Then they had a bottle of ginger-beer each. It was really lovely.

"This is the village of Nursery-Rhyme," said Mary Contrary. "Tom the Piper's Son lives over there – he's a very naughty boy, always being whipped for stealing pigs. I don't have much to do with *him*! Next door lives Jack Horner, but he has a very good opinion of himself – he's always saying that he is a very good boy!"

"Yes, I know all about him," said Mary Brown." Does Humpty-Dumpty live here too?"

"Yes," said Mary Contrary. "But, you know, he's very silly. He's been warned heaps of times not to sit on walls – but he always will. Then he falls off, and as he is a great big egg, he breaks, and there's such a mess to clear up. All the king's horses and all the king's men can't mend him. But he's all right again by the morning – and off he goes to sit on the wall once more!"

"I wish I could see him," said Mary, excited. "This is a lovely place, I think. Does Polly Flinders live here too?"

"Yes, but she's a dirty little girl,"

said Mary Contrary, wrinkling up her nose in disgust. "She sits among the cinders and spoils all her nice new clothes. So her mother has to whip her. There is the Black Sheep here too. He doesn't belong to Bo Peep, though – all *her* sheep are white. She's a silly girl, she's always losing them."

"But they come home all right, don't they?" asked Mary, anxiously.

"Oh yes, and bring their tails behind them," answered Mary Contrary. "Will you have some more ginger-beer? No? Well, now, what about getting you home? I'll walk part of the way with you – and perhaps you wouldn't mind if I gave one of my pretty maids – my dolls, you know – a ride in Josephine's pram for a treat?"

"Of course!" said Mary, getting up and smiling. "I know Josephine would love to have someone in the pram with her."

So Mary Contrary tucked up Esmeralda, her best pretty maid, into the pram beside Josephine, and the two dolls were very happy to be with one another. Mary loved to see her own doll smiling so cheerfully.

Off the two little girls went. Mary looked excitedly at all the little houses she passed. A little girl with a red cloak and hood stood at the door of one and Mary felt sure she was Red Riding Hood. She saw Johnny Thin who put the cat in the

well, and Johnny Stout, who pulled him out. She waved to the Old Woman who lived in a shoe, and wished she could go nearer to the funny old house in the shape of a shoe and look at it. But she was afraid that the Old Woman might think she was one of her many children, and whip her and put her to bed.

At last they left the queer village behind and went into the wood. It wasn't very long before they were on the right path to Mary's home.

"Well, you know the way now," said Mary Contrary kissing Mary Brown. "Do come and see me again, won't you. And be sure to bring Josephine with you."

She took Esmeralda out of the pram, kissed Josephine good-bye, and

stood waving to Mary as she went along the green path. Mary hurried along anxious to tell her mother all her adventures.

Mother *was* surprised! She couldn't believe her ears!

"Well, you shall come with me, Mother, next time I go to see Mary Contrary," promised Mary Brown. "I know you'll love to see everybody!"

So Mother is going with her tomorrow. I DO hope they find the right path, don't you?

Make Yourself a Whizzer

Whizzers are great fun and very easy to make. Perhaps you could have a competition with your brothers and sisters or friends to see who can make the best whizzer of all.

Here's all you'll need:
An empty cardboard box (one that's held cereals or something like that)
Strong thread or fine string
Glue
Pencil
Scissors
Paints or felt tip pens
Saucer

First of all, you'll have to open out your box very carefully and lie it down flat. Now place the saucer on the cardboard and draw round it very carefully with your pencil. Draw two circles like this, then cut them both out. Stick the two circles together, so that you have the plain sides on the outside. When the glue is quite dry you can paint a design on both sides of the cardboard circle with your paints or felt tip pens.

Make sure your paint is quite dry before you try to do the next part, otherwise you'll smudge your pattern. When it is dry, take your scissors and make two holes in your cardboard circle, as shown in the picture. Now thread the fine string through the holes, and tie a knot, so that you have a long loop at either side of the circle. And now your whizzer is complete.

To make it work, you simply swing the cardboard circle over and over so that it twists the string, then pull tight and just watch it whizz round! By pulling the string tight and then letting it go loose you can make your whizzer work for ages and ages without stopping. Try it and see. . . .

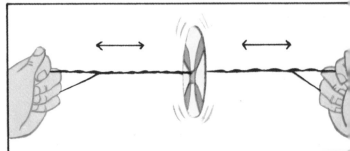

CHOOSE A COLOUR

From Pixie Pippin's palette choose a colour to rhyme with each of the people or objects on the page.

In the King's Shoes

Once upon a time the brownie pedlar Twiddles was sitting down by the lane-side mending a kettle. As he sat there who should come along but the King of Brownie Land himself! He was walking slowly, as if he were tired. He saw Twiddles sitting by the lane-side and he sat down by him.

"Your Majesty, can I run to the nearest cottage and get a chair for you?" said Twiddles, jumping up and bowing.

"No," said the King. "Let me sit in the grass for once if I wish to. My shoes hurt me. I shall take them off for a few minutes while I talk to you."

The King slipped off his beautiful, highly polished shoes with their silver laces.

"My word!" said Twiddles the pedlar, "I'd dearly love to be in your shoes for a little while, Your Majesty."

"You would, would you?" said the King. "Well—it's a silly, foolish wish of yours—but I'll grant it! Get into my shoes—and you'll find yourself king! I'll be a pedlar for a few happy hours!"

Hardly believing his ears, Twiddles got into the king's shoes. They fitted him perfectly. He stood up—and gazed down at himself in astonishment. He was dressed like a king—and the King was dressed like a pedlar! Such was the magic in the King's shoes! Whoever wore them could be the King himself!

"Go down the lane and you'll meet my servants," said the King. "Good luck to you! I'm going to have a snooze

in the shade here and listen to the birds singing."

Twiddles went down the lane, holding his head high and looking as proud as could be. He was King! King! How grand it felt!

He saw some men hurrying towards him.

"Your Majesty, Your Majesty!" they cried. "You will be late for the opening of that sale of work. Hurry, Sire!"

"Dear me," thought Twiddles, "so I am to open a sale of work, and everyone will bow to me and cheer me. How fine!"

He hurried to a waiting carriage and climbed into it. He drove off quickly to the next town. How the people there cheered him! He opened the sale of work, and read a speech that was put before him. He stood in the hot sun for about an hour, shaking hands with all kinds of brownies. He began to feel tired.

"I say, isn't it about time for dinner?" he asked a courtier nearby.

"Not nearly," said the brownie, looking surprised. "You have to review your troops of Boy Scouts next, Your Majesty. Have you forgotten?"

"Oh, well," thought Twiddles, "it will be fun to ask the Boy Scouts all about their campfires and the best way to boil kettles on them. I am sure I could teach them a thing or two about that!"

But, to his surprise, when he began to talk to the Boy Scouts about this sort of thing his courtiers nudged his arm and frowned.

131

with lots of marvellous things to eat and drink!"

But, to his great disgust, as soon as he had finished with the Boy Scouts, he was hustled into his carriage and driven off to see a new ship being launched—and a footman presented him with a little packet of sandwiches to eat!

"Is this all my dinner?" asked poor Twiddles. "Just sardine sandwiches? Well, well, well! I'd be better off if I were a pedlar! I'd at least fry myself bacon and eggs, with an apple or two to follow!"

"Your Majesty, there is no time for you to have a proper lunch to-day," said the courtier who was with him.

"Your Majesty is not supposed to know how kettles are boiled or camp-fires made!" they whispered. "Those are not the sort of things a king is interested in."

"Dear me," thought Twiddles. "How dull it must be to be a king all one's life! How hungry I am getting! Whenever are we going to have dinner? I guess it will be a fine one—

"You have to be at the dock yards in half an hour. And after that you have to visit a hospital. And then there is the flower show to go to."

"Do you mean to say that all these things are on one day?" asked Twiddles in disgust. "Don't I get any time off at all?"

"Your Majesty is acting very strangely to-day," said the courtier, looking troubled. "You promised to do all these things—and a king must keep his promise."

Twiddles launched the new ship. He rushed off to the hospital, and walked round and round the wards, and spoke to every one in the beds there. By the time he had finished, his feet felt as if they could not walk another step, and his face was stiff with smiling so much. He badly wanted a cup of tea.

But no—he had to go to the flower show next, and miss out his tea altogether! He was still very hungry, as he had only had the sandwiches for dinner.

He yawned and yawned at the flower show, and his courtiers looked most disgusted with him. He didn't at all want to see the beautiful flowers they showed him. He didn't want to smell any of them. He just wanted to sit down on a chair and have a cup of tea all by himself.

When the flower show was over he was driven to the palace. Twiddles was thrilled to see it shining in the evening sun. The people cheered him as he passed.

Twiddles forgot about his dull and tiring day and waved his hat to the people. But that was not the thing to do at all. He had to bow stiffly from left to right and from right to left. He got out of the carriage and went up the long flight of steps.

"I want a jolly good meal now," he said to the courtiers.

They looked surprised. "Your Majesty, you will only just have time to change into your best uniform and get ready for the big military dinner you are giving to-night," they said.

"Oh, well," thought Twiddles, "I shall certainly have something to eat at the dinner—and I shall look very

handsome in a uniform, too."

The uniform was tight and stiff. It cut him round the legs. It cut him across the shoulders. It was heavy. But still, he did look very handsome indeed. He went down to the dinner. But before he could sit down he found that he had to shake hands with two hundred guests! Twiddles was not used to shaking hands with so many people and his hand soon ached terribly. At last he sat down to the table.

He had a famous general on one side, and a famous prince on the other. They both talked so much that Twiddles hardly had time to eat anything, because he had to keep saying, "Yes, certainly," and "No, of course not!" almost every moment. The dinner took a long, long time. Twiddles got very bored. He thought the general and the prince were both very silly. He wished they would stop talking for just one minute. But they didn't.

At last bedtime came. Twiddles felt as if he was being squeezed to death in his tight uniform. He could hardly breathe. He was so very, very glad to get out of it. His servants left him when he was ready for bed. He stood and looked at the beautiful bed ready for him—and he shook his head.

"No," said Twiddles. "I don't want to sleep in you—and wake up in the morning to rush about all day long doing things I don't want to do. It's a difficult thing to be a king. I'd rather be a pedlar. I'm free, but a king is not. A king has many masters and must do as he is told all day long—a pedlar has no master and is as free as the air! I'm going back to be a pedlar again!"

He slipped out of the palace in his sleeping-suit. He made his way to the stables. He jumped on a horse, and rode bareback to the lane-side where he had left the king.

There was a small light there—the remains of a campfire. A man was sleeping peacefully beside it. It was the real King. Twiddles woke him.

"Wake up!" he said. "I've come back. I'm not a good king! I got hungry and bored. I'd rather be a pedlar."

The King sat up and stared at him.

"Well, I got hungry and bored, too, when I was a king," he said. "I like being a pedlar. It's lovely! Just do what you like, and nobody to say, "It's your duty to do this or that!" No, Twiddles, you go on being a king. I don't want to go back."

Twiddles kicked off the King's shoes. He had put them on to come back in. In a trice he had changed once again to the untidy pedlar he had been that morning. Even his beautiful sleeping-suit disappeared and he was dressed in his same old clothes. But the King was dressed in the fine sleeping-suit—he was no longer a pedlar!

He got up. "Well, well," he said, "I suppose I had better go back. After all, it's my job. I must do it as well as I can for the sake of my people, who love me. But oh, pedlar, you can't think how I have enjoyed to-day!"

"Yes, I can," said Twiddles, patting the King kindly on the back. "You've enjoyed to-day just as much as *I* shall enjoy to-morrow. Now, good-night, Your Majesty, and pleasant dreams!"

Twiddles lay down by the fire. The King galloped back to the palace on the horse. And when the pedlar awoke next morning he wasn't at all sure that it was nothing but a dream!

"Poor old King!" he said. "He has the hardest job in the world. Won't I cheer him when I next see him! But I wouldn't be in *his* shoes for anything!"

135

Bless my Whiskers!

I love little Pussy, her coat is so warm,
And if I don't hurt her, she'll do me no harm.
I'll sit by the fire, and give her some food,
And Pussy will love me, because I am good.

If you live in the country, spotting wild animals and birds can be lots of fun, but even if you live in the town it doesn't mean that you can't be an Animal Spotter too.

For instance, you could be a bird spotter, even in the town, or perhaps you'd prefer to be a dog spotter, or perhaps a cat spotter.

And to help you get started on your spotting, here are four kinds of cats that you might like to look out for.

BLACK – Long-haired

There are two main types of cats, those with long hair and those with short. Long-haired black cats are quite a rare sight, they are completely covered with jet-black fur from head to toe, without a trace of grey or white, and they have large orange-coloured eyes. You'll have to be on your toes to spot one of these cats.

COLOURPOINT – Long-haired

Colourpoint cats look just like Siamese cats, except that they have much longer hair. Their beautiful coats are cream, but their tails, faces, feet and ears are brown and they have round blue eyes.

TORTOISESHELL-AND-WHITE –Short-haired

The brightly-coloured tortoiseshell-and-white cat is a very easy one to spot because of his beautifully marked coat. Look for a cat with a coat of red and black patches with splashes of white and eyes of either orange, copper or hazel.

RED TABBY – Short-haired

Tabby cats are very popular and there are lots of different kinds, silver ones, red ones and brown ones. And it's the red one that you have to watch out for. Red tabbies have beautiful red coats with even deeper red markings on them in a striped pattern. Their eyes are either hazel or orange. But don't get them mixed up with the ginger and sandy cats, of which there are many, because they're not the same at all.

Happy cat spotting!

Connie's Cousin

Connie's cousin is coming to stay with her for a holiday, and she is very excited because they always have fun together. If you look carefully at all the objects on this page and then take the first letter of the first object, the second letter of the second object, the third letter of the third object and so on, you will find out the name of Connie's cousin.

1

2

3

5

4

6

7

The Little Roundy Man

BILLY, Joan and Tom were out for a picnic in the woods one day when their big adventure happened. They didn't know it was going to happen at all, and it all began when Joan wanted to play hide-and-seek.

"All right," said Billy. "I'll hide my eyes first. Call 'Cuckoo' when you are ready."

He hid his eyes, and waited for the others to shout "Cuckoo." Tom ran behind a big bramble bush, and crouched down. Joan found a hollow tree with a hole just big enough to squeeze through. She got in, and called "Cuckoo! Cuckoo!"

Billy opened his eyes and began to look for the others. He soon found Tom, but didn't catch him, for Tom got home first. Then he looked for Joan.

Now as soon as Joan got into the hollow tree she looked about her, but at first it was too dark to see anything. Then she saw a very queer thing. There was a little shelf in the tree. just about the level of her head – and on it was a pair of little blue shoes!

Joan thought that was very strange indeed. Who would hide shoes in a hollow tree? And who had built the neat little shelf? It was very queer. Perhaps the fairies lived near by and the shoes belonged to them.

Joan began to feel excited. She forgot about the game of hide-and-seek and called to Billy.

"I say, Billy!" she cried. "There's something funny in this tree. Come and see."

Billy and Tom went racing over to look. When they saw the little shelf and the shoes on it they were full of surprise. Billy took the shoes from the shelf, and helped Joan out of the tree. Then all three looked at the shoes.

They were very beautiful, made of the softest leather, and were the brightest blue you can imagine. They had silver buckles on, and when Billy turned the shoes upside down, he saw that they had never been worn.

"Do you know, Joan, I believe they would just fit you!" said Tom. "Do try them on."

So Joan took off her own shoes, and slipped on the blue ones. They fitted her perfectly. She stood up and began to dance about in them – then a funny thing happened.

The shoes suddenly began to walk away with her. She felt her feet being taken down the path that led to the heart of the woods. She tried to turn back to the boys, but the shoes kept

142

her feet going to the middle of the wood.

"Joan! Come back!" called the boys. "Don't go that way! You'll get lost!"

"Help me, help me!" cried Joan in a fright. "I can't come back! The shoes won't let me! Billy! Tom! Come and hold me so that I can't go any further!"

The boys raced after Joan – but as soon as they were almost up to her the shoes on her feet began to hurry, and somehow or other Joan found herself running faster than she had ever run in her life before.

"Quick! Quick!" she shouted to the panting boys, "I'm being taken away. These shoes are magic! Oh, catch me, Billy, and take these shoes off!"

But the boys couldn't catch Joan, no matter how they hurried. In a few moments she was quite out of sight in the dark wood, and soon they could no longer hear her cries for help. They stopped and looked at one another.

"Oh my goodness," said Billy. "This is a dreadful thing! Where has poor Joan gone to? And oh, Tom – we're quite lost! I don't know where we are a bit, do you?"

"No," said Tom, looking all round. "And isn't it dark, Billy? The trees are so thick that not a ray of sun gets through. Oh dear, what *are* we to do about poor little Joan? It's no good going after her – and if we try to get help we shall only get more lost."

"Well, we must do *something*," said Billy. "Look, there's a kind of rabbit path over there. Let's follow that and see if it brings us anywhere."

The two boys went down the narrow, winding path. After a few minutes they came to a curious house. It was perfectly round, and had one chimney at the top. There was a window and a door. and that was all. It was about twice as high as they were, and the boys thought it was the funniest place they had ever seen.

"What shall we do?" asked Billy. "Shall we knock?"

"Yes," said Tom, and he walked boldly up to the door. He knocked loudly, like a postman – rat-a-tat-tat, rat-a-tat-tat.

At once the door flew open and the queerest little creature looked out. He was almost as round as his house, and he wore big round spectacles on his funny daub of a nose.

"Now, now!" he said, crossly. "I thought you were the postman. What do you want?"

"Well, it's rather a long story," said Billy. "But we would be so glad if you would help us."

And he told the little round man all about the shoes that had run away with Joan.

"Dear, dear, dear!" said the little man, and he took his glasses off and polished them ."You'd better come in and sit down. I may be able to help you a little. This is a very serious matter."

The two boys went into the round house. It was the funniest place inside, quite round, with no corners at all. There was one room downstairs

and one room upstairs. Everything was round. The table was round, the stools were round, the carpet was round and the clock was round. There was a cat by the fire and it was almost round too, it was so fat and sleek.

"Now I had better tell you at once that I am afraid those blue shoes belong to Candle-shoe the old Magician. He plays a trick with them whenever he wants someone to help him with his spells. He puts them in a hollow tree or under a bush, and whoever finds them and tries them on is straightaway led to him in his underground cave. Of course, he wants one of the fairy folk, not a little girl – but if he thinks she will do for him, he will keep her for years to help him with his nasty old spells."

"Oh my!" said Billy in a fright. "But whatever shall we do, little man?"

"My name is Roundy," said the little man. "Well, I must see what I can do to help you. I will first find out if Joan has gone to the cave. Half a moment. Hie, Tibby, fetch me the magic basin."

Tibby, the little round cat, at once got up and fetched a basin from a shelf. She filled it with blue water from a jug, and set it on a stool in front of Roundy. He took a peacock's feather and stroked the water gently, whispering a string of magic words all the time, which neither Billy nor Tom could understand. Suddenly the water became still and flat like a mirror. Roundy bent over it and breathed on it. Then he rubbed it clean with a duster.

"Look!" he said. "You can see your sister now!"

Billy and Tom looked into the basin of blue water, and on the mirror-like surface they saw a picture. In the middle was Joan, very tiny, still walking with the blue shoes on her feet. As they watched, she came to a little door in a hillside. It swung open and she walked through a long, long passage, which got darker and darker. Then suddenly she came to a cave, and there in the middle sat Candle-shoe, the old, ugly magician.

Just at that moment the water seemed to cloud over, and the wonderful pictures vanished. Billy and Tom looked at Roundy in despair, for they could not bear to think of poor Joan in the power of that nasty old magician.

"Yes, it's what I thought," said Roundy, emptying the water out of the window. "Candle-shoe has got her. Well, how are we going to rescue her?"

"First of all, where is this cave?" asked Tom.

"Nobody knows," said Roundy.

"But how can we go there, then?" asked Billy.

"Let me think for a moment." said Roundy. He sat down on a stool, put his head in his hands and frowned hard. Then he suddenly snapped his fingers, and jumped up.

"I've got it! Look here, we'll find another pair of old Candle-shoe's shoes and put them on. Then they will lead us to the cave, and we shall know where it is."

"Yes, but the shoes go so fast that whoever is following can't keep up," said Tom.

"Ah," said Roundy, "but I can tell you what to do about that! We'll only put *one* shoe on, and then we shall go slowly enough for us all to keep up. I'll put the shoe on, and you shall follow me."

"But how shall we find out where a pair of the shoes has been put?" said Billy. "We can't go looking in every hollow tree."

"Oh, that's easy enough," said Roundy. "My house will take us to a pair in a twinkling."

"Your house!" said Billy and Tom together. "But how can a house do that?"

"Well, you see, it's quite round," said the little man, smiling. "It can roll along like a ball, and that's how I get about all over the world."

"But what about the chimney?" asked Billy. "That sticks out, you know."

Roundy opened the door and went outside the house. The boys followed him. He gave a big jump and landed just beside the chimney. He pressed hard on it and it sank down into the house, leaving just a hole where it had stood before. The boys were too surprised to say a word.

"Ha," said Roundy, jumping down again. "Mine's a fine little house, isn't it? Now would you like to come inside while my house rolls along, or would you rather follow it, walking behind?"

"Oh, I think we'd rather follow it," said Tom. "We should be so dreadfully bumped about inside, shouldn't we? What about you, Roundy? Do you stay inside when your house goes travelling?"

"Oh yes," said Roundy. "I don't get hurt because I'm quite round, you see. I just roll about like a ball, and so does Tibby. Now wait a moment . . . I want to tell the house where to go."

Roundy leaned against his round house and stroked it as if it were a cat – and to Billy's surprise, and Tom's, it began to purr!

"Little house, little house," said Roundy in a loving voice. "Do you know where Candle-shoe hides his pairs of shoes?"

The house purred more loudly than ever.

"You do?" said Roundy. "That's good. Then take me to one of those pairs of shoes, little house."

He popped inside, and slammed the door. The house suddenly began to roll itself away through the wood, just like a great big ball. Billy and Tom stared and stared – it looked very queer indeed. They followed it. It didn't go very fast, and all the time it rolled it seemed to be humming a song. It was the funniest house the boys had ever seen.

It rolled through the wood, and

came to the open country. Then it came to a river and bounced into the water. Billy and Tom jumped in too and swam across behind the big ball of a house. The house rolled up the bank of the opposite side and stopped. The door flew open and out came Roundy with a duster.

"I must just dry it before it gets a chill," he said to the boys. "Sit in the hot sun for a few minutes, you two, and you will soon be dry."

The boys sat down and dried themselves, whilst Roundy rubbed and polished his funny little house. Then he popped indoors again, and the house rolled on once more.

It rolled until it came to a green hillside. It came to a stop beside a bramble bush. The door flew open and out ran Roundy.

"There must be a pair of shoes somewhere here," he said in excitement. So they all looked hard – and sure enough, Tom soon came across them. They were red this time, quite small, and had silver buckles just like the others.

"Ha!" said Roundy, taking them from Tom. "Now I'll just put one on!"

He popped one on his right foot, and held out his hands to Billy and Tom.

"The magic's working!" he said. "Come on! My house will follow too. It always goes where I go."

The boys each took one of Roundy's fat hands, and went with him. The house followed behind, humming it's queer little song.

"You see, wearing only one of the shoes means that I don't go at all fast," said Roundy.

The shoe took him up the hill to the top, and then down the other side. There was a deep pit at the foot, and a flight of stone steps led down to the bottom. Down went Roundy, and the two boys scrambled behind. At the bottom of the pit was a large trap-door which opened as they came near. They went through it, and saw more steps leading downwards. Soon they were in a long dark passage, lighted here and there by tiny lamps. Down they went and down, right into the heart of the earth – and then up, they came, and up, until at last they could see daylight ahead of them once more.

When they came out of the passage into the sunshine they saw in front of them a very steep mountain.

"That must be the mountain the magician lives in," said Billy to Tom. They made their way towards it, and

when they came to the foot they saw a narrow winding path. The magic shoe took Roundy up and up, and at last the three of them saw a door in the hillside, fast shut.

"Hold me whilst I slip off this shoe," said Roundy. "I don't want to walk into the cave just yet!"

The two boys held tight whilst Roundy pulled off the magic shoe. He tossed it away, and put on his own. Then he sat down and looked round.

"Well, we're here," he said. "The next thing to decide is – how are we going to rescue Joan?"

They all thought for five minutes – and then Roundy began to chuckle.

"I think I know," he said. "I'll

just play a nice little trick on old Candle-shoe. You two hide yourselves and watch."

The boys went behind a bush and peeped out to see what Roundy meant to do. He went boldly to the door in the mountainside and knocked loudly seven times. In a moment the door swung open and the magician himself looked out.

"What do you want?" he said crossly. "Go away or I'll turn you into a grass-hopper."

"I pray your pardon," said Roundy, bowing to the ground. "But see, Your Highness, I have brought a marvellous house for you to see. Maybe you would like to buy it."

The magician looked at the round house which at once hummed its song again and turned itself about for Candle-shoe to see. The magician was astonished.

He put on a pair of enormous spectacles and walked over to the house.

"This is a queer affair," he said to Roundy. "Never in my life have I seen a house like this."

"It follows its owner like a dog," said Roundy. "It will always come if you whistle. It has a pull-out chimney, and a little round cat to sit by the fire."

Roundy pulled the chimney out and pushed it in to show the magician, who was more astonished than ever.

"Now buy it, sir, do," said Roundy. "Think what a surprise it will be to all your friends, the witches, and think how they will envy you."

"How much is it?" asked the magician.

"Only four gold pieces," said Roundy.

"It seems very cheap," said Candle-shoe in surprise. "Is there anything wrong with it inside?"

"No, Your Highness," said Roundy. "Please go inside yourself, and look all round."

The magician pushed open the door and stepped inside. Roundy gave a great shout of joy, and slammed the door at once. He locked it, and then gave his house a push.

"Roll up and down the mountainside!" he commanded. "Give the old magician a shake-up, little house!"

At once the house began to roll up the hill and down, and the magician inside began to yell and shout in fright. Roundy paid no heed, and he and the two boys rushed into the cave and began to look for Joan. They went down a long dark passage and soon came to the place where Joan was, for they could hear her calling.

But alas! The door was locked! Billy banged on it and called to Joan.

"Joanie! Joanie!" he shouted "Are you all right?"

"Oh, Billy!" cried Joan's voice. "Have you come to rescue me? Yes, I'm all right, but I've been frightened because that horrid old magician wanted me to help him with his bad spells and I wouldn't."

"Where's the key to this door?" asked Tom.

"Oh, the magician has got it hanging on his girdle," said Joan. "However can you get it?"

The three outside the door looked at one another in dismay.

"Come on," said Roundy to Billy.

"We'll go and see if we can get it, somehow or other. You stay here and keep Joan cheerful, Tom."

Off went Billy and Roundy. They came out on the hillside and looked to see what the little house was doing. It was still rolling up and down and the magician was still calling and shouting for help.

"Stop, little house," said Roundy. The house stopped, and stood still. Roundy ran up to it.

"Hie!" he called to the magician. "Throw your keys out of the window, quickly."

"Certainly not!" said the magician, angrily. "I'm not going to let you have that little girl back again!"

"Little house, roll faster!" commanded Roundy. At once the little house began to roll around faster than ever and Candle-shoe was bumped about inside in a dreadful manner. He begged for mercy, and Roundy stopped the little house again.

"Where are those keys?" he cried. The magician threw them out of the window, and Roundy picked them up in glee.

"Go on little house, roll around a little more so that Candle-shoe can't get out!" he said, and the house began to roll about gently.

Billy and Roundy ran back through the dark passage to the cave. Roundy fitted the biggest key in the lock and turned it. The door opened and Joan ran out. Billy and Tom hugged her tightly, and Joan began to cry for joy. Then the boys told her who Roundy was, and she hugged the kind little man too.

"Now how are we going to get back?" said Tom.

"Let's look about in the magician's cave," said Roundy. "We are sure to find something or other that will take you back safely."

They looked here and they looked there, and suddenly Roundy gave a shout of joy.

"Here's a witch's broomstick," he cried. "We'll take it outside, and if you all sit on it and wish yourselves home you'll be there in half a shake of a duck's tail!"

"But what about you?" asked Billy, as they ran outside into the sunshine.

"You'll see what happens to me when you're safely in the air on your broomstick!" laughed Roundy "Hop on!"

They all sat on the broomstick, and then Roundy suddenly clapped his hands twice and called out a magic word. The children wished themselves home, and up in the air rose the broomstick at once. The riders held tight, and looked down to see the last of Roundy.

He commanded the little house to stop rolling, and unlocked the door. At once the magician leapt out – but before he could get hold of Roundy that fat little man had hopped inside the door, banged it, and the little house was scurrying away down the mountainside as fast as an express train!

How the children laughed to see it!

"Hurrah for Roundy!" said Billy. "He was a fine friend to us! I do hope we see him again some day!"

Their broomstick flew faster and faster, and at last brought them right over their own house. It flew down into the garden, and the three children jumped off. Billy put out his hand to catch the broomstick and take it indoors to show his mother, but he wasn't quite quick enough – for it flew away from him, and mounted up into the air once more, all by itself.

"There it goes!" said Joan. "Oh, my dears, what an adventure we've had. Quick, let's go in and tell Mummy before we forget anything!"

So in they raced – and Mummy really couldn't believe her ears when she heard all they had to tell!

PIPPITTY'S PET CANARY

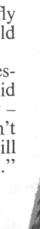

LITTLE Princess Pippitty had a beautiful yellow canary called Goldie. She loved it very much, and looked after it every day. She loved it far better than any of her other pets, and when the King and Queen took her away to the seaside for a holiday she wanted to take Goldie too.

"No, you can't do that," said the Queen. "Goldie must stay behind with all your dogs and cats and ponies. We will ask Gobbo the elf to look after Goldie for you."

"But suppose he lets Goldie fly away!" cried Pippitty. "It would break my heart, really it would."

"Well, if he lets your canary escape, he will lose his head!" said the King. "Now cheer up, Pippitty – you may be sure Gobbo doesn't want his head cut off, and he will look after Goldie very well indeed."

The day came for the King and Queen and Pippitty to start off in the golden coach. Pippitty said good-bye to all her pets, and kissed her canary on his little yellow beak.

"See that you look after Goldie well, Gobbo," said the King. "Feed him every day, give him fresh water to drink and to bathe in, and clean out his cage – and whatever you do don't let him fly away! If you let him escape, off will come your head!"

"I will look after him well," promised Gobbo, and he bowed very low. Then the Princess blew a last kiss to her canaray, and stepped into the golden coach. Off they all went to the seaside.

Gobbo went to the canary's cage every day, and did all that he had been told to do. Goldie fretted for the Princess, and sat all day long on his perch, moping. Gobbo tried to cheer him up, but it was no use.

"Where's the Princess?" Goldie kept asking. "Where's Pippitty? Let me out, Gobbo, and I will go and look for her."

"Oh no, I mustn't let you out," said Gobbo. "Be patient, Goldie. Pippitty will be back soon. I should lose my head if I let you out of your cage."

The time went by, and at last came the day when the Princess Pippitty was to come back home again. Gobbo went to Goldie's cage and cleaned it out beautifully. Then he polished the bars till they shone like gold.

"You haven't given me enough water to bathe in," complained Goldie. "I shall tell Pippitty when she comes back."

"Pippitty is coming back to-day," said Gobbo.

"Oh, I don't believe you!" said the canary. "You have kept saying she would be back soon, she would be back soon, and she didn't come. Give me some more water to bathe in."

Gobbo opened the door of the cage, and he was just going to put some more water in, when someone at the door called: "Gobbo! Gobbo! Come quickly and see the rainbow!"

Gobbo put the water down quickly and ran to the window – and alas, he forgot to shut the cage door! In a trice Goldie was out of the cage and flying round the room. Gobbo shut the window with a bang, and then ran to shut the door. The canary could not get out of the room.

Gobbo's friend, Peepo, the one who had told him to look at the rainbow, stared at Gobbo in surprise.

"What are you shutting the doors and windows for?" he asked. "Do you feel cold?"

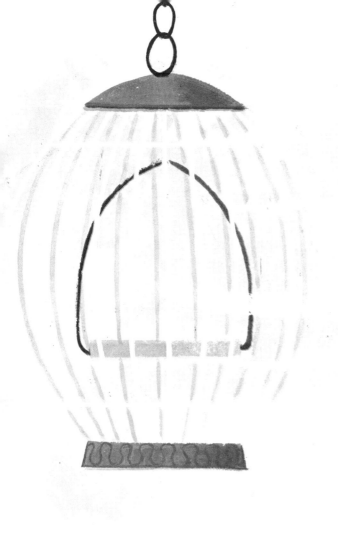

"No," said Gobbo, "but don't you see that Goldie the canary has escaped? I shall lose my head if the Princess comes back and sees him out of his cage."

"Oh my, oh my!" said Peepo in dismay. "Do go back to your cage, Goldie."

"Not I!" said Goldie. "Once out of my cage I'll never go back! I'll just wait till the Princess comes and then I'll fly down to her shoulder and ask her to let me be free."

"You would die if you flew out of doors like the other birds," said Gobbo. "You don't know how to find your own food. Be a sensible little bird and go back to your beautiful big cage."

But Goldie wouldn't. Gobbo began to cry, for he felt quite certain that his head would be cut off when the King and Queen returned. Peepo sighed in despair, for he knew that if only he hadn't called Gobbo to look at the rainbow his friend wouldn't have let the canary escape.

Suddenly there came a knock at the door and in came Merry-one the Jester. The canary flew to the door to get out, but Merry-one shut it just in time.

"Hallo, hallo!" he said in surprise. "What's this I see? Goldie out of his cage! I fear you will lose your head for this, Gobbo."

"Oh, Merry-one, help me to get Goldie back!" begged Gobbo, the tears running down his cheeks.

"How did he get out?" asked Merry-one.

"Well, you see," said Gobbo, "I was just giving Goldie some more water, when Peepo called out to me to go and see the rainbow, and while I was looking, Goldie –"

"Wait a minute, wait a minute!" said Merry-one, looking puzzled. "I'm getting muddled. Now, let's begin again. Goldie was giving Peepo some water, and you saw a rainbow ?"

"No, no," said Gobbo. "*I* was giving Goldie some water, and Peepo called out –"

"Where was Peepo?" asked Merry-one, looking more puzzled than ever. "Was he in the cage?"

"No, *I* was in the cage, you stupid creature!" cried the canary.

"Oh, *you* were in the cage," said Merry-one. "Well, Peepo was giving you some water, and Gobbo called out to him to see a rainbow, and –"

"No, no, *no*!" said Gobbo and Peepo together. "You've got it all wrong."

"You *are* a stupid fellow!" said the canary, fluttering its wings crossly. "Begin at the beginning, now. I was in the cage."

"Yes," said Merry-one. "I was in the cage – no, no, that's wrong, of course. Gobbo was in the cage, and Goldie was – no, that's wrong too. Oh my, I'm getting so muddled I shall never, never understand this!"

"I'll *make* you understand!" cried the canary in a rage. "Look here, you foolish fellow. *I* was in the cage – like this –" and Goldie flew back into his cage, and stood on the perch. "Do you understand that, Merry-one?"

"Perfectly, thank you!" cried the jester, and he banged the cage door shut. "*You* were in the cage, Goldie, ha, ha! And you are in the cage now! Ho, ho! Oh yes, I understand all right and so do the others, I'm sure!"

"Ha, ha!" roared Gobbo and Peepo, joyfully. "Oh, Merry-one, we thought you were being so stupid, and really you were as clever as could be!"

"Oh thank you, thank you for saving my head for me!" said Gobbo, and he shook Merry-one gratefully by the hand.

Goldie the canary flew into a terrible rage and shook the bars of his cage till they rattled – but nobody took any notice. They had heard the sound of cheering outside.

"The Princess! The King and Queen!" cried Peepo and Gobbo, and they rushed to the window. Sure enough, there was the golden coach, and as the three watched, the King and the Queen stepped out, and little Princess Pippitty followed.

And the very first thing she did was to rush upstairs to see Goldie her canary! Wasn't it a good thing he was safely back in his cage? He was so delighted to see Pippitty that he forgot all about his bad temper, and sang her a beautiful song of welcome.

Nobody told tales of Gobbo, so his head was quite safe – but dear me, didn't he have a narrow escape?

The Two Friends

Mister Brownie sits at night
In his little house,
Listening to his radio
With his friend the mouse.

They sit and smoke without a word
In dressing-gowns of blue,
(The mouse's has a nice big hole
To let his tail come through).

Their pipes are acorn-cups, of course
They pick them up each day
From underneath the oak that grows
Along the woodland way.

They go to bed at ten o'clock,
And curl up warm and tight;
Mister Brownie, Mister Mouse,
We wish you both goodnight!

The JACK-IN-THE-BOX

IN the toy shop there lived an ugly old Jack-in-the-Box. He had sticking-up hair, a big nose, staring eyes and a horrid laugh. He loved frightening the other toys, and was always ready to jump out at them.

It was all right during the daytime, because then he had to stay in his box and keep quiet unless the shop-keeper undid the lid. Then he would spring right up into the air with a nasty squeak, and all the toys near by would shiver with fright.

But at night he used to get out of his box and jump about on the shelves. He hid behind the doll's house and jumped out at the fairy doll. He frightened her so much that she ran straight into the fire engine and tore her lovely frock.

The toys became very tired of the Jack-in-the-Box. They never knew when he would jump out at them,

nor what he would do next. So one night, when he was for once asleep in his box, they held a meeting about him.

"Perhaps the clockwork train would take him right away somewhere," said the fairy doll.

"No, I wouldn't," said the train. "I'm not going to have anything to do with him. He jumped out at me last night and made me run off my rails and break a wheel."

"What about the motor-bus or the fire-engine?" asked the golliwog. "Wouldn't they take him away somewhere and lose him?"

"Yes, but even if we did take him," said the motor-bus, "how can we make him get out if he doesn't want to? He'd just stay in his seat and we'd have to bring him back again."

Then the aeroplane on the top shelf spoke.

"*I* don't mind flying off with him,"

it said. "I can turn upside down when I'm flying, and I could tip him out, and fly straight back here."

"Oh good!" said the toys. "Well, how shall we manage it?"

"I'll give each of you rides to-morrow night," said the aeroplane. "The Jack-in-the-Box is sure to want one too, and as soon as he is safely in the seat I'll fly out of the window!"

So the next night all the toys took turns at having flights round the room in the aeroplane. It was great fun and they enjoyed it. Then suddenly the Jack-in-the-Box jumped out at the golliwog and scared him so much that he fell into a bowl of water and nearly got drowned.

"Now Jack-in-the-Box, stop your tricks and come and have a ride!" cried the aeroplane, landing just by Jack.

Jack-in-the-Box wrapped his muffler round his neck and climbed into

the pilot's seat. The aeroplane rose into the air and flew straight out of the window.

All the toys cheered and clapped their hands when they saw the horrid Jack being taken away. They waited and waited for the aeroplane to come down and Jack dropped out and fell right down the chimney! The witch was sitting by the fire, and she jumped up in fright when she saw Jack coming down the chimney.

"She shouted some magic words at him, and changed him into a

back – and when it did, they crowded eagerly round it.

"What did you do with him?" they asked.

"Ha!" said the aeroplane. "You'll never guess! When I was flying over a witch's cottage I turned upside mouse! I know, because I circled round and peeped through the window. When I saw what she had done I landed and waited till the mouse came running out, frightened of the witch. It jumped into the pilot's seat, and I brought it here!"

"What! You've brought Jack, that horrid Jack back again!" cried the toys in horror.

"Oh, he's only a mouse now, very much scared, and full of shivers!" laughed the aeroplane. "Just look at him."

The toys peeped into the pilot's seat. There at the bottom, trying to hide, was a tiny mouse, trembling and afraid.

"Ha, now Jack knows what it is to be frightened!" said the toys. "This is a good punishment for him!"

The little mouse was taken out of the aeroplane, and he at once ran to hide himself in a corner. The toys

were, sorry for him, and took no more notice of him. But Cinders the shop cat, smelt him, and was soon lying in wait for him round every corner.

The poor mouse was always being pounced on, and only just managed each time to escape with his life. Now he knew how dreadful it was to be jumped at and frightened. How he wished he had'nt been unkind to the toys before!

One night the mouse crept into his old box for shelter, and fell asleep there. When he woke up – lo and behold, he was no longer a mouse! He had changed back to his own shape. He was a Jack-in-the-Box again!

The toys were sorry and frightened when they saw what had happened. They were afraid that all their terrors would begin again. But the Jack-in-the-Box had learnt his lesson. He was gentle and kind, and never again did he jump out at any of the toys and scare them.

"You must forgive me for all my past unkindness," he said. "Do let me be friends with you."

So the toys forgave him, and now they are all as friendly as can be.

And the only time that Jack ever leaps out of his box is when Cinders the cat comes by. She jumps in fright, and then Jack laughs loudly. He hasn't forgotten how she frightened him when he was changed into a tiny mouse.

PETER'S NOAH'S ARK

PETER had a lovely play-house at the bottom of the garden. He kept all his toys there, his soldiers, his fortress, his teddy bear, his golliwog, his books and his beautiful Noah's Ark with all its animals and birds.

Just outside the play-house was a little stream, and Peter often used to sail his big boat, his two little boats and his steamer there. He had great fun.

One day his cousin John came to ask if he would go to spend the night with him, and bring all his boats and his steamer.

"I've got a fine pond in my garden," said John. "We'll sail our boats and have a splendid time."

So Peter went to his play-house and took all his boats. Then he shut the door and off he went with John. The toys felt rather sad, for they knew that no one would play with them that day.

"I do hate it when Peter goes off and leaves us," said the bear. "There's nothing much to do."

"Toys never have adventures like boys and girls," said the golliwog. "We just stay here and do nothing unless Peter plays with us. Oh, I *would* like an adventure, wouldn't you?"

"Rather!" cried all the soldiers.

Mr. and Mrs. Noah looked out of the ark.

"Perhaps one day we shall all have a fine adventure," they said.

"Pooh!" said everyone, rudely. "*You*'re not likely to have adventures with your silly old ark!"

Mr. and Mrs. Noah said no more. They knew they were old-fashioned, and they often felt hurt when the other toys laughed at their wooden ark.

But that night an adventure really *did* come to the toys! For just about midnight they heard a great shouting outside, and woke up in a fright. Then someone came knocking at the play-house door.

"Open, open, in the name of the King of Fairyland!" cried a voice.

The teddy bear ran across the floor and opened the door. Outside stood an elf, wet through and dripping.

"Oh!" he said. "Such a dreadful thing has happened. The King and Queen of Fairyland were going along in their ship down the stream, on a visit to the Prince of Buttercup Land, when suddenly a wind came and blew the ship right over!"

"Good gracious!" cried all the toys in horror. "Are they drowned?"

"No, nobody's drowned," said the elf. "But we're all wet through, and the ship has sunk. We want to know if we can come in here and dry ourselves."

"Of course," said the toys. "Of course! Oh dear, we are dreadfully sorry! We will light the fire in the old dolls' house and you can dry yourselves there."

The soldiers ran to the dolls' house and opened the front door. They quickly lighted the fire in the drawing-room, and then one of them started the kitchen fire too, and put a jug of cocoa on the stove to warm.

Soon in came the King and Queen, wet through and shivering. They were delighted to see the bright fire, and very soon they were sitting by it, drying themselves. Their little elfin servants dried themselves by the kitchen fire, and poured out tiny cups of hot cocoa, which they took to the King and Queen.

"We are very sorry to hear of your sad plight, Your Majesty," said the teddy bear. "We wish that you could spend the night in the

dolls' house, but unfortunately there are no beds. Peter gave them all to a little girl friend of his one day when she came to play with him."

"Dear, dear, what a pity!" said the Queen. "But anyway, I'm afraid we musn't stop after we have dried ourselves. We must get on with our journey, or the Prince of Buttercup Land will be very much worried about us."

"Perhaps there is a boat here we might borrow?" asked the King.

"Oh, Your Majesty, Peter has taken both his big boat and his little boats to his cousin's," cried the toys in dismay.

"Well, is there a toy steamer we might have?" asked the King.

"Peter's taken that too!" said the golliwog. "Oh, Your Majesty, what ever will you do?"

"Well, really, I don't know," said the King. "There is nowhere here we can sleep for the night, and nothing we can continue our voyage in. It is a real puzzle!"

Then suddenly Mr. and Mrs. Noah walked up to the King and bowed stiffly, for they were made of wood.

"Your Majesties!" they said, politely. "Would you care to borrow our wooden ark? We can easily turn out all the animals, and make it comfortable for you. It is watertight, and will float very well indeed."

"I have sometimes heard of a Noah's Ark," said the King, "but I have never seen one. Let me look at it. The Queen and I are almost dry now."

So they walked out of the dolls' house and went to see the Noah's Ark. All the toys went too, and most of them were very cross with Mr. and Mrs. Noah.

"Fancy offering to take the King and Queen in your stupid old ark!"

NOAH'S ARK

they whispered to Mr. Noah. "Whatever were you thinking of?"

But Mr. Noah took no notice. He led the King over to the ark, and the Queen went with Mrs. Noah.

"Well!" said the King in surprise. "So that is a Noah's Ark! It looks big enough to take us all quite comfortably, much better than a small boat. It is really very kind of you, Mr. Noah, to offer to lend it to us. Would you come with us to steer it? I don't think any of my servants know how to guide an ark."

"Certainly, certainly," said Mr. Noah, blushing with delight. All the toys were most surprised, and said never a word. The King called his servants and showed them the ark.

"Shall we get in now?" he asked.

"I must first get all the animals out," said Mr. Noah. "They live there, you know, two of each kind."

Then he clapped his hands and called to the animals. They all pushed up the lid and looked out to see what was happening.

"Come out!" cried Mr. Noah.

"The King and Queen of Fairyland want to borrow the ark for a little while."

Then out tumbled all the wooden animals, and walked up to the King and Queen two by two and bowed. Their Majesties were delighted, and thought they had never seen such polite animals before.

"Now, Your Majesty, I'll just borrow a ladder from the toy farm," said Mr. Noah, "and you and the Queen can climb into the ark. Ho, soldiers, fetch some comfortable chairs from the dolls' house for their Majesties to sit in!"

The soldiers scurried off and came back with chairs. The golliwog fetched the ladder from the toy farm, and Mr. Noah put it against the side of the ark. In a trice the King and Queen and all their servants were safely inside, sitting on their chairs.

Then ropes were tied to the ark, and the soldiers hauled on them. The ark slid across the floor and out on to the grass. Soon it was by the stream, and then, with a gentle

splash, it was launched. All the toys cheered and waved good-bye. The wooden ark animals had marched down to the water in twos, and the King and Queen laughed to see them.

Off sailed the ark down the stream in the moonlight. It went right away to Buttercup Land, and the Prince was full of astonishment to see it.

"Thank you so much," said the King and Queen to Mr. and Mrs. Noah. "We don't know what we should have done without you and the wonderful ark. Please come and see us. We will send you an invitation when we get back to Fairyland."

Mr. and Mrs. Noah said good-bye, and guided the ark back home. They were simply delighted to think that they had been able to help their Majesties. As for all the toys in the play-house, they couldn't make enough fuss of Mr. and Mrs. Noah.

"We *are* sorry we laughed at the

ark," they said. "*Do* tell us all your adventures!"

And dear me, when the invitation came from the King and Queen to a moonlight party in Fairyland, for Mr. and Mrs. Noah and all the wooden animals, what an excitement there was! And how envious all the other toys were!

Mr. and Mrs. Noah didn't need to go in the ark, for the elfin messenger said he could take them a short cut down the garden path, and along a passage in a hollow oak-tree. So off they all went.

Mr. and Mrs. Noah went first, feeling ever so proud. Then came all the animals in twos. It really was a sight to see! I should love to have gone with them, wouldn't you?

FLOWER PICTURES

Here are six pictures which should remind you of six flowers. Are you clever enough to guess their names?

The Lazy Giant

THERE was once a giant called Sleepyhead who was dreadfully lazy. He couldn't be bothered to do his housework, he couldn't be bothered to mend his clothes, and he never worried about adding up his money or paying his bills.

"I think I shall go and live in Fairyland," he said to his friends one day. "There I can make the pixies do all my housework for me, and my shopping, and I'll make them mend my clothes for me too! They shall keep my accounts and I shan't have anything to worry about at all!"

So he packed up his things, ordered a horse and cart to take his furniture, and set off. What a commotion there was in

"There's some work for you to do now," he called to the fairies. "You'll have to mend your bridge!"

They were very angry, but they could do nothing, for the giant was so enormous that he could put a hundred fairies in his pocket at once.

At last he arrived at an old castle which had once been built by an enchanter. He went inside it and decided that it would just do for him, though it was a bit on the small side.

"Hi, you pixies!" he called to some small fairies who were sitting on the castle wall, watching in astonishment the giant coming in and out of the castle, carrying his furniture, "come along here and do some work for me!"

The pixies jumped down from the wall and ran away, but the giant leaned over the wall and caught them one by one in his big fingers.

"Now!" he said angrily, "you just do as you're told! Come along into my castle and clean it up."

Fairyland when he arrived! For one thing, the horse and cart were giant ones, and the fairies fled in terror when they saw such great big things coming along their small roads. The cart broke a bridge when it went over a river, and the giant laughed.

Poor Pixies! They had to start work at once, and Sleepyhead kept them going all day long with brushes, mops, and pails! He made them go out and get something for his meals, and they even had to cook for him. Then he brought out a great pile of dirty clothes and ordered them to wash them the next day, and mend them.

Well, it wasn't long before Sleepyhead had everything in his castle quite perfect, for he kept about a hundred pixies there, working for him day and night. They did not dare to run away, for he threatened to go out of his castle and trample down their pretty little village if they played any tricks on him.

But how they grumbled and groaned and cried and sobbed! It was dreadful to have to work so hard for a great unkind giant.

"If only we could get rid of him!" sighed the pixies. "But how can we? We don't know enough magic to make him leave. He will be here for always."

The pixies did everything for the giant – except just one thing. And that was, they could not do his accounts for him! They were no good at adding and taking away, and as Sleepyhead was even worse, his money was soon in a dreadful muddle.

"I don't know what bills I've paid

and what I haven't!" he raged one day. "I don't know how much money I've got, nor how much I've spent! Lazy, stupid little things you are! Fancy not being able to add up my figures for me!"

"Well, why don't you do them yourself?" said Peeko, a cheeky little pixie who was the only one who dared to speak up for himself.

"Because I always fall asleep in the middle of my adding up!" roared the giant. "That's why! And don't you talk to me like that, Peeko, or I'll put you into my flour-bin and keep you there for a day. You'll be a fine sight when you come out!"

"What you want is something that will add up your figures for you!" said

Peeko. "*We* can't do it, but I believe there is a machine that can add figures. I have heard of one, I know."

Sleepyhead pricked up his big ears.

"Oho! That is just the thing for me! I will buy one. I should like an adder, then all my shopping lists could be added up correctly without any mistake, and my money could be added properly too. Get me an adder from Giantland, Peeko. Order one at once!"

"But they may not keep such things," said Peeko nervously, rather sorry now that he had mentioned anything about an adding-machine.

"How dare you tell me about something that they may not keep!" thundered the giant, in a very bad temper. "Write off at once to Giantland, and tell them to send the biggest adder they've got at once. And for a punishment for being cheeky, you shall lick the stamp yourself, Peeko!"

This was certainly a dreadful punishment, for the giant stamp was as big as a large picture, and it took an enormous lot of lick to get it properly stuck on a giant letter. Still, Peeko didn't dare to say he wouldn't do what he was told. So he took his pen and wrote a letter:
"To Giantland Shops, –

"Please send at once a box containing the largest adder you have, addressed to Sleepyhead Giant, High Castle, Fairyland.

"Yours faithfully,
"Peeko."

Then he had to spend an hour licking the very large stamp to stick on the very large envelope. After that he took the letter to the post, carrying it on his head like a muffin-man carries his tray. It wouldn't go into the pillar-box, so Peeko had to leave it at the post office.

Two days later there came an answer:

"To Sleepyhead Giant, –

"Your letter received with thanks. We are sending you the largest adder we have, as soon as we can get it. Please treat it carefully.

"Yours faithfully,
"Giantland Shops."

"There you are!" said Sleepyhead, in delight, showing the letter to Peeko. "You see, they *have* got an adding-machine. And you see that they say, 'Please treat it carefully.' That means we shall have to oil it well and see that it is kept clean and bright. That shall be your job, Peeko. Get in a big bottle of oil, and six new dusters. And if I ever see a SPECK of dust on my adder, I'll put you in my ink-pot!"

In three more days a large box arrived carried by a giant messenger, for it was too big to send through the pixie-post. The giant was delighted. His adder at last! He took it from the messenger and called Peeko and all the other pixie servants.

"Come here!" he cried. "Here is my new adding-machine! Now all my shopping accounts and my money will be added up correctly, and I shall never have mistakes made again! You shall all come and see it, for a treat."

The pixies came into the kitchen and climbed up on chairs and tables to see the wonderful new machine from Giant-

land. It was in a long box that had big holes down the sides. The giant placed the box on the table and began to cut the rope that bound it.

Suddenly a strange hissing noise came from the box. "SS-ss-ss-ss-ssssssssss!" The pixies looked startled.

"What's that noise?" said Peeko, going pale.

"Oh, I expect it's the machine beginning to work or something," said Sleepyhead, cutting another rope.

"SS-sss-ssss-sssssss!" Peeko leapt off the table in alarm, and all the other pixies scrambled down to the floor.

"It sounds like a big snake!" whispered Peeko. "Quick! Go into the room upstairs! We will lock ourselves in, in case it is a giant snake!"

All the fairies ran helter-skelter up the stairs and soon locked themselves into the room there. They were trembling with fright. Peeko listened. The giant was roaring in anger.

"Where are you going to, you pixies? Come back! You wicked little things, running away like that! Wait till I get you! I'll just open this parcel and then I'll come after you!"

"SS-ss-ss-sssss!"

Sleepyhead ripped off the lid of the box, and out glided a great, slippery adder! It was an enormous snake, with

TO SLEEPYHEAD GIANT

wicked eyes and a long, black forked tongue that flashed in and out as the snake looked around the giant's kitchen.

"Oooooh! Ow! It's a snake! It's a snake!" yelled the frightened giant. "What have they sent me a snake for?"

Peeko suddenly began to dance about in glee in the room overhead.

"He asked for an adder, and they've sent him an adder — but they thought he meant the adder snake, and not an adding-machine! Oh joy, joy, joy! He'll have to run away, or the snake will get him!"

The great snake looked at the giant, and it didn't like his thundering voice at all. It made a dart at him.

"Ow! It's going to bite me!" cried Sleepyhead in a great fright. "Peeko, Peeko! Come and take it away!"

Peeko opened the door a crack and yelled back: "Run, Giant Sleepyhead, run! The snake will bite you to death if

you don't! It's an adder! Run! Run!"

The snake darted at the giant again and he opened the kitchen door and rushed out, his enormous boots making a great clattering on the stone yard outside. All the pixies ran to the window to see him. The snake glided out of the door after him. Sleepyhead took one glance round and howled dismally:

"It's coming, it's coming!"

He leapt right over the castle wall and raced up the hill that led out of Fairyland back to Giantland. The snake glided swiftly after him. The pixies held their breath and watched the race. The snake could go very quickly indeed, and it was full of fierce anger after being shut up in a box for so long.

The giant reached the top of the hill and went over the other side, with the adder still after him. Then both were out of sight, but the pixies could hear for a long time the sound of the giant's great, noisy footsteps going farther and farther away.

"Well! He's gone at last!" said Peeko, delighted. "Now, what about having this castle for ourselves? It would be fine to give dances in!"

So the pixies took the castle for themselves, and how they laughed when they thought of the giant sending for an adder to do his sums for him – and getting a snake instead!

As for Sleepyhead, nobody knows if he raced the snake or not. Perhaps he is still running away, with the adder close behind him. It would really serve him right, wouldn't it?